A
Harlequin
Romance

WELCOME

TO THE WONDERFUL WORLD

of Harlequin Romances!

Interesting, informative and entertaining,
each Harlequin Romance portrays an appealing
love story. Harlequin Romances take you
to faraway places — places with real people
facing real love situations — and
you become part of their story.

As publishers of Harlequin Romances, we're extremely
proud of our books (we've been publishing
them since 1954). We're proud also that Harlequin
Romances are North America's most-read
paperback romances.

Eight new titles are released every month and are
sold at nearly all book-selling stores across
Canada and the United States.

A free catalogue listing all available Harlequin Romances
can be yours by writing to the

HARLEQUIN READER SERVICE,
M.P.O. Box 707, Niagara Falls, N.Y. 14302.
Canadian address: Stratford, Ontario, Canada.

or use order coupon at back of book.

We sincerely hope you enjoy reading
this Harlequin Romance.

Yours truly,

THE PUBLISHERS
    Harlequin Romances

WAYAWAY

by

DOROTHY CORK

HARLEQUIN BOOKS   TORONTO
WINNIPEG

Original hard cover edition published in 1972
by Mills & Boon Limited, 17-19 Foley Street,
London W1A 1DR, England

© Dorothy Cork 1972

Harlequin edition published December 1972

SBN 373-01644-1

Printed in Canada

CHAPTER ONE

KEITHA GODWIN and her brother Martin had been holidaying in Cairns for almost a week. Today they had taken the launch out to one of the coral islands and spent the morning drifting over the reef channels in a glass-bottomed boat.

The beautiful flower-like coral with its delicate tints, the gorgeously coloured tropical fish, and the hypnotically waving tentacles of the sea anemones had fascinated Keitha. Her thoughts had gone to Donn, back in London, and she had wished that he were there beside her under the palm-thatched awning of the long flat boat. It was dreadful being away from Donn—far worse than she had imagined it would be when she had decided to fly out to Australia to stay with Martin for a while in Queensland. But if she wanted Donn to realise just how much they meant to each other, this, she was sure, was the best way to do it. Absence was supposed to make the heart grow fonder.

Now, hundreds and hundreds of miles from London, she and Martin were lunching at the Coral Reef Hotel Restaurant, and while she enjoyed her meal of reef fish and salad, and talked to Martin of the pleasures of the morning, her eyes were continually—almost compulsively—drawn to a party of four at a nearby table. Everyone in the restaurant was in holiday gear and these were no exception, only their clothes had a subtle air of being exclusive—of being resort wear rather than simply holiday clothes. There were two pretty blonde girls, obviously sisters, and a fair-haired young man who must surely be their brother. The fourth member of the party was entirely different. He was older, somewhere about Martin's age, definitely over thirty, with a strong jaw and brown hair very much bleached by the sun. He had a rangy, rather ruthless sort of look about him, and his fashionable shirt with its pink and mauve print design on an ivory ground, unbuttoned almost to the waist, was in contrast to his masculinity.

He looked a tough sort of man. Leaning back in his chair smoking, eyes narrowed, a half smile hovering over his mouth, he sometimes talked, sometimes listened to his companions. But at all times he had about him a curious air of command. It was while she was speculating about him, wondering what niche he would fit into in life, rejecting the city as his milieu, rejecting after no more than a moment's hesitation the sugar cane fields of the north, that she missed what Martin was saying to her.

The waitress had brought their coffee, and Martin, pouring cream, had a slight frown on his pleasant face. He was a good-looking man, his eyes, very dark like her own, framed by square dark-rimmed glasses.

'Come on now, Keitha,' he adjured. 'Smarten yourself up. Where were you? Back in London with that television producer who's doing his best to ruin your life?'

Keitha blinked with annoyance. This was the first time Martin had shown any sign of interfering in her affairs. Up till now, all he had cared about was that she should eat, sleep and soak up some sunshine; lose the dark shadows that were around her eyes and get a little more flesh on her bones. It was a pretty serious thing, in his eyes, to be suffering from overwork at the age of twenty-two!

Of course she had known that fussy little Aunt Jane would tell tales and write Martin all about her. But she had taken it for granted that her brother would concede that she knew what she wanted. He had always been kind and tolerant and uninterfering. She remembered that well, although he had left England eight years ago when she was still a schoolgirl.

Now she sent him a warning look that said—she hoped—'Don't interfere', and she told him lightly, 'Actually, I was trying to work out how those people over by the window fit into the social pattern here.'

Martin turned his head, and Keitha caught the eye of the older man for the first time. Sardonic, aware, he tilted an eyebrow at her. She noticed as she looked hastily away that his eyes were of a peculiar fiery blue.

'I've met those two girls in Townsville. Good to look at, aren't they?' said Martin approvingly, turning back to her with a smile. 'They're from Brisbane—name of Warner—their father's an architect. I made up some opal jewellery for them last year—haven't seen them since. I might see what I can do about that.'

Keitha allowed herself a little smile. Martin saw only the girls, whereas it was the man who intrigued her.

'To return to our conversation,' said Martin. 'Tell me one thing, if you can, Keitha. Why are you so set on getting yourself tied up with Donn Gorsky? Aunt says he's too sophisticated for you by half, and even I can see that working for him is too demanding for a girl of your constitution. You don't really want to marry him, do you?'

'Yes, I do,' said Keitha. 'I want it more than anything else in life.'

Martin drummed on the table with his fingers. 'I take it he hasn't asked you to marry him yet, then?'

'Not yet,' said Keitha. She gave him a straight look. 'Donn belongs to a crowd that doesn't believe in marriage. He wants me to—to shack up with him.' She looked at her brother warily, watching for his reaction,

7

but he was not shocked, merely annoyed.

'You turned *that* offer down, of course?'

'Yes, of course. But only because I *do* believe in marriage'

'Well, that's something,' said Martin dryly. He signalled to the waitress to bring them more coffee, and Keitha was suddenly conscious that the man at the table by the window was studying her. A slight turn of her head and she met his gaze—speculative, intense. For some reason the colour rose in her cheeks and she thought with annoyance, 'What is he staring for? How rude can you get?'—forgetting that a few minutes before she had done *her* share of staring. She turned deliberately away from him and back to Martin, who said thoughtfully,

'You were always a determined little puss. Has it ever struck you that you quite frequently miscalculate the value of what you want in your determination to get it?' He paused while the coffee was poured, then continued. 'You were a pretty child, with those great dark eyes and your fair delicate complexion—you still are. In my opinion, Aunt was too soft with you—sorry for you, I suppose, because you were an orphan. I remember one school holiday when I was sixteen or so. Aunt took us to lunch in London. You couldn't have been more than four years old. You refused milk, and demanded water—but you wanted sugar in it. You got it finally.' He smiled wryly at Keitha across the table. 'You didn't like it—I can still see the face you made!—but you drank it. Every bit of it.'

'I don't remember,' said Keitha, smiling faintly. 'But what's the moral?'

'Simply that there are girls who will hold out for what they *think* they want, and when they get it, it often doesn't suit their taste at all. You're one of those girls.'

'If you're trying to prove something about Donn,' said Keitha, annoyed, 'then none of this is relevant. We're in love. I'm not making a mistake there, Martin. And all that was a long time ago. I'm not like that any more.'

'No? Let's refresh your mind with something more recent, then—your job as assistant to a television producer. You went all out for that when even I—who haven't seen you for quite a while—could have told you it would be too much for you. It's a job that needs a thick skin, a logical mind, and the constitution of an ox. You possess none of those attributes, and it's not surprising you eventually broke down under the strain.'

Keitha shrugged. 'You're exaggerating. I enjoyed the work. It was a challenge. I'd go back to it—and I probably shall.' She looked at him coolly. It *had* been exhausting work. The hours were irregular and there were so many things for which she had been responsible—studio bookings, instructions regarding sets and costumes, notifications of rehearsal times, the shooting script to be retyped overnight if changes had been made during the day. She had stuck to it mostly because of her boss, Donn Gorsky. When she had been a secretary, he had noticed her, and arranged for her to be his assistant, and of course she had fallen over herself to make a success of the job. She might not have the constitution of an ox, but she had ambition and determination and tenacity. She wouldn't have tossed in the job even temporarily if the doctor hadn't been so adamant that she needed a long spell. She had turned it to her own advantage by coming right away to Queensland. It was a move designed to force Donn to a reassessment of their future relationship, and she fully believed it would bring a different proposal from him—one of marriage. Particularly if she showed signs

9

of falling so in love with Martin's tropics that there was some doubt as to whether she would come back to England at all...

Martin said, 'Well, that brings us back to what I was talking about when you fell into your daydream. I was proposing that instead of going back to your old job, you stay here and work for me. One of the girls in the workroom is leaving to be married in a couple of weeks. With those long sensitive fingers of yours and your artistic flair—I remember that from when you were a kid—you might like to try your hand at jewellery fashioning and designing. As you know, opals are my speciality, and if you like a challenge, you have it there.' He smiled at her in his open friendly way. 'So how about it?'

'No, thank you,' said Keitha blithely. 'I really don't need to be cajoled and wheedled on to the path of morality and righteousness, Martin. I have a very level head and I know exactly what I want and what I'm about.'

He looked exasperated. 'That's your opinion of yourself. Aunt appears to think it's open to conjecture. And though I haven't met Donn Gorsky this I know— you're becoming rather a handful, and Aunt isn't getting any younger. I wish you'd think about it.'

Dear Martin! He pictured himself taking her off Aunt Jane's hands. She gave him a sympathetic smile. 'All right. I'll think it over this very afternoon.'

'Good girl! Finished your coffee?' He pushed back his chair. 'I suggest we go down to the Underwater Observatory now. I can guarantee you'll be more than fascinated.'

Keitha followed him out into sunshine that was slashed with shadow from the tall palm trees. 'I think I've seen enough underwater life for one day, Martin. You go if you want to, and I'll lie on the beach and sunbake and think upon my sins.'

He sent her a reproving look. 'Think about my suggestion instead,' he amended. 'All right, I'll pick you up later on.'

Twenty minutes later Keitha had changed into her brilliant orange swimsuit of ribbed cotton and was lying on glistening white sand in the shade of a huge green and white umbrella. Back from the beach, coconut palms rustled softly and soporifically in the warm wind, and in the water holidaymakers cruised lazily in boats or waded in the clear green shallows searching for shells or exploring the coral reef.

Keitha lay there for a long time. Mostly she thought about Donn, but some of the time she thought about Martin's proposition. She thought of the opals she had seen in his jeweller's shop in Townsville. Black opals, water opals, milky opals—beautiful and fascinating, all of them. Some were from Lightning Ridge in New South Wales, some from the Coober Peedy fields in South Australia. Others were from the lesser-known fields of outback Queensland—Martin had fossicked for those himself. But while she thought it might be fun designing settings, the idea didn't really excite her. Now if Martin had suggested a week or two in the opal fields that would have been different altogether.

At all events, she had an uneasy feeling that Martin was now all too ready to play the big brother and deafen her with advice. For all she knew, he might even have some young man lined up in Townsville as opposition to Donn. But it was no go. She was mad about Donn—but she had no intention of shacking up with him. It was marriage or nothing. She was going all out to get that proposal from him—and she rarely failed to get what she wanted. In her letters to Donn, she wrote gaily of the wonderful time she was having in Queensland, of how she was revelling in the sunshine. She didn't mention the future and she didn't mention marriage. That was going to irk Donn, sooner or later. His own letters were full of longing for her; she really mattered to Donn—it was plain in every line he wrote. If it was a battle to see who could hang out the longest for their principles, she knew who would win. Donn would finally have to realise that some things hadn't changed so drastically since 'that funny little maiden aunt of yours' was a girl.

The thought made her smile to herself, and his face floated tantalisingly before her closed eyes—lean, intelligent, his hair thick and wavy and dark, his eyes——

She gave a start and opened her own eyes guiltily. Donn's eyes were smoky grey—they weren't that light and penetrating blue. Where had she seen eyes like that recently? Of course—that man in the hotel restaurant who had stared at her so rudely!

She put her head down on her arms again, noting that she was acquiring a faint tan. She could feel the sea breeze gently lifting the silky dark brown hair from her bare shoulders, and presently she slept lightly...

She woke to hear the soft sound of footsteps crunching on the sand close by. 'Martin,' she thought, and turned her head lazily without bothering to open her eyes. She said dreamily, 'I've thought about what you offered, Martin, and it's very attractive, but the answer's definitely no. I shan't pretend—I haven't the slightest intention of spending the rest of my life in sunny Queensland.'

No reply. She opened her eyes and sat up slowly. The man who stood looking down at her quizzically was not her brother at all. He wore blue swim shorts, his torso was deeply tanned, and his eyes, narrowed against the glare from the white sand, were a vivid electric blue.

He was, in fact, the man who had occupied her attention at lunch time. For a full five seconds she stared at him and he stared back. His brows, heavy and straight and sunbleached, were lowered. She was uncertain whether or not he was smiling, but the mouth above the jutting aggressive chin had an upward tilt at the corners, and there was a distinctly sensual look about it that unnerved her.

He shifted his weight and looked her over—the full slender length of her in the high-necked orange swimsuit. Instinctively she groped for her sunglasses and curled her legs beneath her. With the merest quirk of a smile that was wholly and stunningly masculine, he drawled out,

'What sort of way is that to talk to a stranger? Especially to one who's not used to taking no for an answer. I'll guarantee *I'd* soon make you say yes, so for your own sake I hope Martin is easier to reckon with.'

She felt her cheeks stain with colour that rapidly ebbed away. Of course he was joking and she should laugh and pass it off lightly, but her heart was hammering, and there had been something oddly and reasonlessly shocking in the way he had said '*I'd* soon make you say yes'. She decided she didn't like it, and as well, she had, as Donn would have put it, lost her cool. So she turned her back on him and pulled her white beach coat over her shoulders.

'I'm not in the least interested in what you hope,' she told him coolly.

His low laughter was genuinely amused and irritated her more than it would have done. If he had any sense, he'd realise she wasn't the sort of girl who took to being picked up by a stranger—even anywhere as informal as on a coral island. But he didn't go away. He said, 'Given just a little time, we could surely

13

change that, too.'

Keitha's annoyance was increased. She didn't like people who were so confident of changing the opinions of others. She began to collect her belongings, and to wish that Martin would come. After a minute she turned cautiously around. That maddening man was halfway down the beach. She leaned forward, elbows on her knees, chin in hands, watching until he plunged into the water and swam out with powerful strokes.

Well, that was that. She gave a rueful laugh. Maybe she was losing her sense of humour! She wondered exactly what sort of an 'offer' he thought she had refused. All the same, to say *he* would make her say yes—change her views—that was going too far. Obviously he liked to be the boss, and was both arrogant and conceited...

Martin was a long while about coming to find her, and finally Keitha grew tired of waiting on the sand and wandered up into the shade of the palm trees. It was there that they met up again. Martin was looking very pleased with himself and admitted that in the Underwater Observatory he had renewed his acquaintance with the two Warner girls, and met their brother, whom they had seen in the restaurant.

'And the other man?' Keitha queried.

Martin shrugged, not interested. 'They'd parted company with him, whoever he was. We've an invitation to visit them in their bungalow up the coast on the mainland tomorrow,' he added. 'You'll come, won't you?'

Keitha said she would. She decided not to mention her own little adventure on the beach. After all, there was really nothing to tell.

But as they drove up the coast the next afternoon she couldn't help wondering if she would encounter the 'boss man', as she called him in her mind, at the bungalow. It was possible. And she would snub him if she did ... She was wearing an attractive cotton dress in bright blues and greens—jewel colours were her favourites—and Martin had complimented her on her appearance.

'You're beginning to look really fit again already. Shouldn't be too much to take on a job again in a couple of weeks' time.'

'I quite agree,' said Keitha. 'But don't *you* make plans for me, Martin. You may think of me as your kid sister, but I've been a working girl for quite a while now, and I can look after myself.'

'Well, the job's there if you should change your mind,' he said lightly, and during the drive, to Keitha's relief, he left the subject strictly alone. He was most probably occupied thinking of the Warner girls!

The road up the coast wound through fields of sugar cane and through tropical rain-forest. Staghorns and orchids grew in the treetops. The scent of frangipani was heavy in the air, and hosts of brilliantly coloured birds chattered incessantly. Beyond a high headland, Martin turned down to a beach where the sun struck glitter off a sea whose sapphire waters surged gently against dazzling sand and the salmon-pink of granite rocks. It was here that the Warners were holidaying in a charming white bungalow with cool tiled floors and airy bamboo furniture. The girls were Angela and Julie, and Keitha met them and their mother. The brother, Tony, was not there and neither was the 'boss man'. Keitha was surprised and annoyed at her feeling of letdown.

After lunch they went down to the beach to swim, but presently Keitha left the others and came to sit on the sand with Mrs Warner, who sat back in a canvas chair leafing through a magazine. Lying in the sun,

Keitha lapsed into one of her favourite daydreams about Donn, imagining he was here beside her on the hot white sand, listening to the palm leaves whispering, watching the yellow banana birds with their red eyes, and the bright parakeets that flew among the trees. She thought of dancing with Donn in the warm moonless tropical night—of walking by the sea with him, washed by the soft languorous air ... She moved restlessly, and sat up hugging her knees, her eyes dark and wide.

Mrs Warner closed her magazine and smiled down at her.

'I hope you're not bored, my dear.' Her voice was gentle and attractive. She was a pretty woman, small and fine-boned, her hair a soft silvery blonde that looked—and probably was—natural.

Keitha smiled back. 'No, I'm not in the least bored, Mrs Warner. I don't think I've ever been bored in my life! I hope you don't think me rude—I was almost asleep. I've been sleeping a lot out here—I'm sort of convalescing, though I'm strong as a horse now.'

'I'm glad of that. I gather from your accent that you haven't been here as long as your brother. I hope he's showing you more of Queensland than the coast. Have you been up on the tableland?'

'Yes. We drove up to Lake Barrine and Malanda for a couple of days. We did quite a tour, and I loved it.'

Mrs Warner nodded approvingly. 'Such lovely rainforest! I used to adore to go there when I was a girl. I was brought up outback in the Gulf Country on a cattle station called Wayaway. My father named it—you can guess why! My nephew Dane Langley owns it now. I haven't been back since I was married, which is a long while ago. You're a city girl, I suppose?'

'Very much so. My only experience of country life

16

has been school holidays on my uncle's farm in Devon. I loved riding there. But I lived mostly in London, and worked for a television producer there. I've had to take a break for health reasons and have been revelling in the life out here. My brother's trying to persuade me to stay and work in his jewellery business in Townsville.'

'If that doesn't appeal and you're wanting a job you should have no worries. There should be plenty of positions open to an attractive, intelligent girl like you—temporary or otherwise.' She frowned faintly. 'I have a rather difficult position to fill. I've been commissioned to find someone to give a hand to a girlhood friend of mine at the outstation of Wayaway. It's something of a worry to find someone whom Patty will like and who will at the same time not be averse to life on a remote cattle station. I'm afraid I shall have it hovering around me like a black cloud till we go back to Brisbane and then my life will be plagued by interviews. Quite frankly, I don't believe it's worth a great deal of my time, either. Patty complains of loneliness and will finish by coming over to the coast to live, I'm sure.'

The others came out of the water then, and no more was said on the subject, but strangely it was one that captured Keitha's imagination. A remote cattle station. It sounded romantic—exciting—different. Like nothing she had ever known before. Much more enticing than a jeweller's shop!

The moment she woke the next morning in the hotel at Cairns, there was the idea fully formed—opening like a flower in her mind. She would offer herself for that job on the cattle station! Why not? She was sure she could get it if she set her mind to it. She could stay until Donn had decided he couldn't do without her and wrote asking her to marry him. How

17

long would that take? A month? She didn't think that was being too optimistic. And while she was waiting, she would be seeing another side of Queensland.

She had a letter from Donn in the morning mail. 'All I can think of is when you'll be back,' he wrote. 'Life without you is sheer hell, and I mean that, darling. My new assistant is horribly organised and efficient and as insensitive as a lump of wood. She's a machine rather than a person, and she smiles and smiles and wins every battle with anybody. So swallow down your vitamin pills or iron tablets or whatever they're feeding you on and come back, and I promise I'll shield you from all nerve-shattering encounters in the future...'

No talk of marriage yet. Still, it was in many ways a comforting letter. The thought of that new assistant had worried her a little and given her the occasional nightmare.

'What's the news from London?' asked Martin, joining her by the hotel pool where she sat reading her letter.

Keitha shrugged. 'Nothing much.'

He took one of the gay fibre-glass chairs near by and lit a cigarette. 'I wish you'd change your mind about working for me. You needn't start work right away, you know—though you're looking considerably better than you did when you arrived out here.'

'I'm feeling wonderful.' She gave him a direct look. 'But don't keep on at me, Martin, I'm definitely not going to work for you. I know very well that you're trying to get me into what Aunt Jane calls a more wholesome world to make me forget Donn. That's what this is all about, isn't it? But it will all come right, you'll see. It's only a matter of time.'

'Then you're just going to give yourself a big long holiday in the sun, are you?'

'That was the idea—the doctor's idea,' she added wryly. 'But I think I shall take on a job.'

'But not with my outfit? I thought, being your brother—— Oh well, when we go back to Townsville I'll see what else I can dig up for you.'

Keitha shook her head. 'No—I think I may have found something for myself.' She smiled at his look of surprise. 'A job on a cattle station.'

Martin stared. 'How on earth did you get on to something like that?'

'Oh, I put in some good work with Mrs Warner while you were frolicking in the sea with those two pretty daughters of hers,' she said lightly. As she spoke she recalled for no apparent reason her disappointment at not meeting again the man from the coral island, and she wondered fleetingly who he had been. 'An old friend of Mrs Warner's needs a sort of companion or helper at the homestead. Of course I haven't presented myself as a candidate yet, but I'm pretty sure I shall be able to have the job for the asking.'

'Sugar and water,' said Martin cynically. 'It's a perfectly idiotic idea and I'm certain Mrs Warner will knock you back very smartly.'

'Want to bet?' Keitha's dark eyes challenged him. She was quite determined to get that job.

'Helping on a cattle run probably means cooking for a dozen hungry stockmen—and waiting on all the idle women at the homestead. Supervising the children's correspondence lessons—being at everyone's beck and call. Where is this cattle station, by the way?'

'In the Gulf Country,' said Keitha. 'Wherever that may be.'

'Hmm. South of the Gulf of Carpentaria. Flat unending plains, sizzling heat, not enough water till the Wet comes, and then too much of it.'

'Have you been there?' she asked aggressively.

'No, but I've heard about it. I have no desire to live there. Like you, I'm pretty well geared to city life.'

'It wouldn't be a case of *living* there,' argued Keitha. 'I'm sure I should enjoy the experience anyhow, and I needn't stay long.'

'I'd give you a week.' His eyes ran over her delicate features and slender shoulders, and he laughed suddenly. 'You're a mad sort of a girl. You turn down a job in a jewellery business because you think I'm trying to woo you away from your sophisticated London life, yet the next moment you go all out for becoming some sort of drudge in the tough world of the Gulf Country. You won't like it, you know. However, I'm certain you won't even get a chance to try it...'

As it turned out, her brother was quite wrong.

The next day she took the bus up the coast—for Martin refused flatly to aid and abet—and went to see Mrs Warner. The older woman was very much surprised at the purpose of her visit and at first inclined to take her interest lightly.

'You're a charming girl, but I don't think—I really don't think—you are the right sort of person for the job.'

'Why not?' asked Keitha frankly. They were on the balcony of the bungalow, sipping long iced drinks in the shade of huge mango trees and watching the hypnotic surge of the brilliant sea on the sheltered beach below.

'Why not? Oh well—because you're a London girl—you wear up-to-the-minute clothes, you're obviously used to living at high speed.' She stopped and made a wry face. 'You're just not right for a cattle run, that's all. Too young. You'd be cut off from all the diversions you're used to—you'd be bored.'

'I told you the other day I was never bored. I meant that. I'm sure I should enjoy the life. That is——' she hesitated and went on with a smile, 'my brother is convinced I'd be expected to cook for a dozen brawny stockmen. I don't know how well I'd cope with *that*.'

Mrs Warner laughed. 'Oh dear me, no! You wouldn't have to do anything like that. The fact is that Patty Drummond's husband died last year and she's finding life a little difficult without him. She's lonely. Her daughter Melanie has finished school now, but she's out on the run all day—she's one of those girls who's happiest in the saddle—and I imagine that Patty needs companionship more than help. No, as far as I know there'd be no really hard work entailed. All the same——' She stopped and looked at the girl beside her speculatively.

'All the same——?' Keitha prompted. 'Please, Mrs Warner—I've set my heart on going to Wayaway. Couldn't I at least be given a trial? I'd pay my own fare—and it would interest me so much to see an outback cattle station.'

To her amazement and delight, Mrs Warner gave in suddenly and charmingly. 'Well, if you're really eager to try your hand—it would save me a great deal of trouble. All right. I don't really see why not. Let me see—the mail plane goes out to Wayaway in two days' time. You could fly out and see how you fit in. If it isn't a success, you can simply fly back the following week and I'll see the employment agency when I return to Brisbane as originally planned. Will that suit you?'

'Wonderfully! I just knew you'd give me a chance.'

'I hope we shan't either of us regret it,' the older woman said a trifle dryly.

Before she left, Mrs Warner wrote Keitha a letter of introduction, while the girl waited on the balcony with its polished quarry tiles and bamboo furniture. The bungalow belonged to her nephew, Mrs Warner had said when Keitha remarked how attractive she found it—the one who owned the Wayaway cattle run. Keitha wondered what kind of a man he was and whether she would see much of him, since she was to be at the outstation, whatever—and wherever—that was! Presently the older woman rejoined her and presented her with an envelope, addressed not to Mrs Drummond but to Dane Langley.

'Never mind that they're not expecting you,' Mrs Warner said. 'That doesn't matter in the outback. They're used to unexpected arrivals. Lots of pretty girls go there on all sorts of excuses! If I send a telegram it will be read over the radio and everyone in the Gulf Country will be gossiping and wondering about you. And that's not what we want at all, is it? Especially as you're going more or less on trial——'

Keitha agreed that it was not what they wanted, though she rather wondered who was being referred to. Did Mrs Warner mean herself and Keitha? Or did she mean herself and Patty Drummond and this nephew, Dane Langley?

She wondered too why it was that lots of pretty girls went out to Wayaway—on all sorts of excuses!

CHAPTER TWO

MARTIN was still very sceptical about the whole business two days later when he saw her off on the plane. He was convinced she would be back the next week, and Keitha was equally convinced that she would not be.

The DC3 carried freight and mail across the table-land to several remote cattle stations, stayed overnight at a town on the Gulf, then returned to the east coast. The front of the aircraft was filled with crates and packages, and behind was a variety of passengers, among them five American tourists, all women, and all intent on seeing something of the outback. Keitha was seated next to one of them.

She watched with interest the country over which they flew, and listened carefully when the freight officer answered questions put by the tourists, thinking of the letter she would be able to write to Donn, telling him of her experiences in the fabled outback.

Once they had left the coastal plain with its lush green fields of sugar cane and belts of darker tropical rain-forest, it was not long before the whole aspect of the land changed. Finally the brilliant greens gave way entirely to dull greens and browns, and about an hour after take-off the first homestead showed up on the slopes below. Keitha knew a sense of excitment as the plane came down on the station airstrip. One of the passengers—a well-dressed elderly woman who was on a visit to relatives—got ready to leave the plane as it taxied to a stop in a whirl of dust. The traffic officer opened the rear door and soon had a set of folding steps in place. A Land-Rover arrived, freight was carried down the passage-way of the aircraft and unloaded. A mail bag was handed over and another one taken on board. The pilot and co-pilot exchanged a few words with the man in the Land-Rover, and in ten minutes the plane was on its way again.

Another hour of flying, a ten-minute put-down at a tiny town that sweltered in the sun, and they were flying over the great flat plains of the outback. For the first time Keitha felt a faint tremor of doubt at the wisdom of what she was doing. Glittering white salt pans showed up on the red-brown earth, the vegetation became tough and stunted. The rivers were no more than chains of waterholes strung out like necklaces across the bosom of the land. In the Wet, the traffic officer told them, those watercourses would be flooded and the earth would be covered with rich and beautiful green pastures, and the cattle would grow sleek and fat and shining...

There was another small town, more cattle stations, and then Tyrone Park, which Keitha knew was the last set down before Wayaway, some twenty minutes further on. The Americans were fanning themselves. 'My, it's hot,' remarked the woman next to Keitha. 'I wish I had your figure and then I wouldn't feel it so. You look as cool as a lettuce leaf!'

At the Tyrone Park airstrip, a pretty girl in a pink silk shirt and white jeans sprang out of the station car and came to talk to the pilot while the freight was unloaded. She was slim, and had long light brown hair that had an unusual silvery gleam in it, and Keitha could hear her voice quite clearly.

'Tell Dane Langley I'm coming over to Wayaway after the border muster if not before, and Mellie had better watch out!' There was laughter and determination in her voice. 'One of our little band of adoring females is going to break down those impenetrable defences of his one of these days, and who knows, it might be me!'

'Oh, come off it, Dusty,' the pilot said good-humouredly. 'It's not to every man's taste to take a wife. Dane Langley's a hard nut to crack. Why don't you forget about him and go back to the coast? You're not all that hooked on the cattle country, are you?'

'I could be—under the right circumstances. Besides, nothing venture, nothing win.' She laughed again, but her laughter had a brittle note in it.

'There's a lovely feeling of camaraderie here in the outback,' remarked Keitha's companion. 'I must note it in my journal...'

Keitha missed anything else the girl called Dusty said, and now she was walking back to the car. Keitha could see she had a full soft mouth that looked a little wilful, and that her skin was golden rather than brown. She wondered if they would meet when she came to Wayaway, and she thought of what had been said about Dane Langley and found that for some reason she was prejudiced against him. Which would not do.

Twenty minutes later she looked down on the Wayaway homestead and outbuildings ranged by a huge lagoon on the empty plain below. Wayaway was certainly remote! The homestead was set among dark trees in a long rectangle of garden. She didn't know what the other buildings were, and wondered if one of them might be the outstation.

The airstrip was some three miles from the home-stead. A cloud of red dust raced along the track as the aircraft came down, and by the time they landed it had resolved itself into a Land-Rover, and had pulled up alongside the plane.

At the sight of the man who climbed out—tall and tough-looking in narrow-legged cord trousers and checked shirt, a broad-brimmed hat tilted back on his head, Keitha's heart gave a jolt.

'So I was right,' she found herself thinking, unable to take her eyes off that strong-jawed face with its startling electric blue eyes. She had not once *consciously* thought that Dane Langley, Mrs Warner's nephew, might be the man she had encountered on the coral island, yet somewhere inside she had known it. She thought of the letter of introduction in her handbag and wondered what sort of reception she would get from him. Excitement and a readiness to assert herself rose in her strongly. Not that his reaction mattered very much. She was here to work for Mrs Drummond —at the outstation. She moved to the top of the steps at the rear door, knowing that he had not yet seen her.

'Hi, Dane,' said the traffic officer with a grin, confirming her belief.

'Hi, Jim,' he dawled. At that instant his eyes came up and met Keitha's and she smiled faintly at his little shock of surprise.

'We've got the art materials Miss Langley ordered and——' The traffic officer broke off, because Dane Langley stood, thumbs hooked through his narrow leather belt, staring at Keitha with a half-humorous, half-disbelieving expression on his tanned face. 'Oh, and here's a pasenger for you—Miss Godwin.'

Keitha came down the steps. She thought Dane Langley might have smiled at her, but he didn't. He screwed up those disconcerting eyes and stepped forward. His fingers closed lightly on her slim upper arm.

'Well, Miss Godwin! You've surprised me. Come along and sit in the Land-Rover while I get this business completed and I'll be with you as soon as I can.' No smile, no questions, just a searching acute look from his fire blue eyes.

'Thank you.' Keitha spoke coolly, pleasantly, and walked the few dusty yards with him aware of an odd shiver of excitement. He saw her into the front seat of the Rover and she put on her sunglasses as he strode back to the plane. She wondered if *he* was the reason why so many pretty girls came out to Wayaway, and hoped he did not think she was another of them!

She watched the freight being unloaded—not much of it, the mail bag seemed to be the main item. Dane Langley had strolled up to have a word with the pilot, and Keitha wondered if the message from the girl called Dusty would be faithfully relayed to him. The freight officer brought the mail bag and two cartons over to the car, and heaved out the station mail bag.

'Have a good time,' he said to Keitha. He was a nice young man with a friendly grin, and Keitha knew from his speculative look that he was curious about her. She smiled at him and said, 'Thank you for the flight. I enjoyed it.'

'How long are you staying on Wayaway, Miss Godwin?'

Her smile deepened. 'I don't really know.'

Dane Langley came back, receipts were signed, and then they were off along a bumpy track that led to a gate. Behind them, the small aircraft taxied down the dusty runway and was airborne.

'Well, Miss Godwin, so you decided to put me to the test, did you? I'm amazed at your ingenuity. You must tell me how you worked it.' He drove fast and expertly, and considering the condition of the track managed to look at Keitha fairly frequently.

'How I worked what? What test?' she asked, confused.

'Come now, we haven't had so many conversations you don't recall the challenge I threw out—and that you so solemnly refused to take up? How did it go, now? Didn't I threaten that in no time at all I could have you caring pretty keenly about my opinions?'

'Did you?' said Keitha haughtily. 'I'm afraid I *don't* remember. I'm sorry to disappoint you.' How conceited can you be? she wondered, and felt furious that he should connect her coming here with himself and what he must consider his irresistible appeal. 'I'm right in supposing that you are Mr Dane Langley?'

'Sure I'm Dane Langley,' he said easily. 'And you know it.'

'I didn't know it until today. I have a letter of introduction to you from Mrs Warner. I've come out to help Mrs Drummond.'

'Good God!' Now she really *had* surprised him. 'Aunt Grace sent you along!' A look of intense amusement crossed his face fleetingly. 'How on earth did you manage that? You certainly are quite a girl, Miss Godwin. I'll admit your tactics have knocked me out.'

'I don't know what you mean by tactics,' said Keitha with annoyance and exasperation.

'No? Well, all things considered, if you were so keen to come to Wayaway it would have been a lot simpler to get Aunt Grace to send you out as a guest. Plenty of the girls do it that way and we all have a lot of fun.'

'I'm sure you do,' Her voice was icy. 'But I'm not interested in fun. I'm here to take up a position.'

He laughed softly. 'Can you possibly be serious? It's incredible!'

Suddenly, Keitha was intensely aware of his nearness to her. At the same time her mind began to whirl and she couldn't think clearly. Disconcerted, she gazed out at the country they were passing through. There was an immense impression of vastness, the plains seemed to go on for ever, painted in dull olive and brown and straw colours. The grasses were tall and paper dry, the trees stunted and ancient-looking, and over all was the huge almost colourless sky. She had the weird sensation that she and this Dane Langley who was somehow not quite a stranger were alone in a no-man's-land, driving to nowhere.

They bumped along over a yellow grassy plain that was broken by patches of eucalypts and acacias. Ahead, a heavier line of trees marked the wide, dried up course of a river, with spreading sandy banks. Red-brown mounds taller than a man appeared frequently among the trees, and she realised presently that they were termite mounds—anthills. A flock of rose-crested white cockatoos flew screeching into the air as the car passed by, and she watched them swarm across the sky, then settle again.

In control of herself once more, she turned to the man beside her and asked politely, 'Will you please take me straight to Mrs Drummond? After all, my business is with her, not with you.'

He gave her a sardonic look. 'Honey, anyone who comes to Wayaway has business with me some way or another.'

'Not me,' said Keitha obstinately. 'I shan't be working for you.'

'Well, that too's a debatable point.' There was an edge of laughter in his voice that irritated Keitha, who was determined to make him take her seriously. They had emerged from the belt of trees, and some way ahead she could see the string of long low white buildings and the fenced yards that she had glimpsed from the air.

'Is the outstation here?'

'Honey, you haven't done your homework. The outstation's fifty miles away.'

'Oh!' Keitha knew a sense of shock. Fifty miles away! How was she to get there?

'But don't let that set you back,' the man beside her

continued laconically. 'Patty Drummond's away just now—staying with friends over at Mary Creek.'

Keitha sank back against the leather seat with a sudden feeling of despair and exasperation. What a mix-up! It looked as though her job was for the time being non-existent and under the circumstances she could hardly go back to the coast and come out again in a few days' time!

'Now keep calm, you'll be taken care of and we'll all enjoy ourselves. We like company now and again, Kate and I—if it's the right sort.' Kate? Who was Kate? Keitha wondered. But at least it was another woman— and she would not be here alone with Dane Langley.

'You can hardly blame me for being a little sceptical about this job business, you know. I got the impression the other day that you were pretty keen to get away from—sunny Queensland, didn't you call it? And by the way, did you persuade Martin to take no for an answer?'

'Martin is my brother,' said Keitha coldly. She turned her head away, indicating that personal questions were not going to be encouraged.

'You must tell me about it some time. I like to know all I can about the people who come to Wayaway. By the way, I'll have that letter when you're ready.'

'Certainly.' Keitha took it from her handbag.

They were approaching the outhouses now and past them, almost hidden behind tall dark-leafed trees that Keitha recognised as mangoes, was the homestead, tucked away in its garden and surrounded by a white railed fence. The Land-Rover spun along a well-defined track and pulled up on a gravelled square near a long white building that had a loading ramp in front of its verandah. As she climbed out of the car, Keitha felt distinctly helpless. She had come all this way to a job she knew virtually nothing about, to work for a woman who wasn't even here, and when she was, it would be fifty miles distant. Moreover, this man Dane Langley was not taking her seriously, and even assumed she had come here because of him. Her mind groped towards the thought of Donn, and that just now was no comfort at all.

Dane Langley held out his hand for Mrs Warner's letter and said, 'Now stop looking so completely lost, Miss Godwin. Those great dark eyes are going to swallow me up in a minute. I promise that Kate and I shall take good care of you.'

Keitha blinked, making a desperate effort to release herself from the magnetism of his gaze. She heard a screen door swing open and slam shut in the building behind her, and turning saw a youngish man come on to the verandah and stand there, a cigarette in his mouth. Thick wavy brown hair falling across his forehead reminded her vaguely of Donn.

'Unload the stuff, will you, Bill?' Dane Langley called. 'I'll be with you later.' He took Keitha's arm and they headed for the homestead garden.

Wayaway homestead was white-walled and red-roofed, and looked cool in its setting of green trees and garden. Bougainvillea, its oddly angled papery flowers a deep and vibrant crimson, cascaded from a trellis at one side, and pink and white oleander blossoms breathed their musky perfume along the path. Beyond the garden, a windmill rose against the cloudless sky. Keitha climbed three steps to a wide shadowy verandah and Dane showed her into a big comfortable room with a polished floor and hand-loomed scatter rugs of thick soft cream and tobacco brown wool.

She was reassured by the woman who came forward to meet her—a grey-haired woman of statuesque build, with a slow calm way of speaking, a mouth and eyes that were used to laughter, and a very obvious respect and admiration for the owner of the Wayaway cattle run. Dane introduced her as 'Miss Kate Langley—my housekeeper, backstop and comforter. Kate and my father were cousins, and she has been at Wayaway ever since I can remember . . . Kate, Miss Godwin appears to be Aunt Grace's answer to my request for someone for Patty.' The irony in his voice underlined the unlikeliness of the situation. 'Will you look to her comfort while I read Grace's letter?'

'Of course, Dane. Sit down, Miss Godwin, and I'll see if Lena has the tea ready and get her to set out an extra cup. Dane, did my art materials arrive?'

'They did, darling. Bill's unloading the freight now. In one moment I'll fetch them for you.'

Keitha sat down, Kate excused herself and went off to the kitchen, and Dane stood reading the letter. When he had finished, he folded the pages carefully and made a wry face. His eyes flicked over Keitha—her dark hair, her delicate face, her long slender legs. Kate came back into the room and Lena—a slim aboriginal girl in a neat blue overall—followed with a loaded tray which she placed on a table near the wall.

Dane Langley waited till she had gone, then said, 'Well, knowing how Grace hates putting herself out for anyone, I suppose I might have expected this. But was it so much to ask? I set out my requirements most meticulously in legible handwriting. All she had to do was put the thing in the hands of an agency in Brisbane and sit back. Then—a couple of surely quite painless interviews, the final choice made—after all she knows Patty inside out—and the thing would be over.' He moved across to Kate who was pouring the tea, handed a cup to Keitha and took one himself and drank down at least half of it scalding hot. Kate Langley looked at him in silent sympathy, and Keitha thought fractiously, 'What's so wrong with me? And who does he think he is to decide offhand that I will not do?' For that, very plainly, was the tenor of his song.

He gave another sardonic look in her direction and continued, 'So she has the bright idea of being rid of the whole box of dice in double quick time by sending along a sexy, trendily dressed girl who looks as though she'll blow away in the first puff of wind—and probably will!—and whose only probable interest in the job is that it will give her a good look at the inside of a cattle run...'

'Now, Dane,' said Kate, gently, cajolingly.

Keitha, her cheeks scarlet, looked for words that would put him in his place. His reference to her as a sexy, trendily dressed girl was rude in the extreme and totally unfair. Before she could think of a thing to say, he had finished his tea, put his cup on the table, and told her uncompromisingly, 'Of course you must stay for now, and we'll entertain you. But I'm afraid you'll be back on that mail plane next week. You're not what I ordered at all.'

This utterance delivered, he strode from the room, and Keitha heard the wire door bang as he went outside.

Kate said mildly, 'What a pity, dear. Never mind, you will enjoy your week with us. Dane knows it's Grace's mistake and doesn't blame you.'

'Isn't it up to Mrs Drummond to decide whether I'll do or not?' asked Keitha, holding on to her temper. 'I'm quite sure I'll be able to please her.'

'Well, Dane knows best in these things. We must leave it to him.'

Leave it to Dane Langley! That was something Keitha had no intention of doing. She wasn't going back on the plane next week, with Martin waiting at the other end to say 'I told you so'! She was going to work for Patty Drummond if it killed her. And she would wait for her to return if it took a hundred years.

Presently Kate showed her to a bedroom that opened on to the verandah, and left her there to unpack and freshen up, for by now her luggage reposed just inside the door of the room.

'Please excuse me—I must open my parcel,' said Kate Langley, and with a smile she hurried away.

Keitha stood at the door of her room and looked across the wide shady verandah to the garden. Through the trees, a long way off, she could see the sails of a windmill and the silver gleam of water, which must be the long lagoon she had seen from the air. The bedroom itself was wide and airy with slightly old-fashioned furniture and fresh flimsy curtains, and there was a modern bathroom along the hallway. She bathed her face and changed into a sleeveless yellow blouse and matching skirt. Kate would presumably be busy with her art materials, Dane Langley with the mail, so she decided to take a walk around on her own. She might as well make the most of her freedom until Mrs Drummond returned. She would have plenty to tell Donn, and if Martin was imagining her toiling away in an immense kitchen, then he couldn't be more wrong!

She slipped her bare feet into the red linen shoes she had bought for the beach, tied back her hair with a red ribbon, and walked around the verandah. She encountered Dane Langely at the screen door near the front steps.

'You've forgotten your hat, honey,' he drawled.

She looked at him warily and he laughed.

'Weren't you going to have a look around? Fetch your hat and I'll come with you. That way you'll see a lot more.'

That was true enough, so she did as he said and

reappeared in a flimsy red straw with a wide dipping brim and ties to keep it in place, and he screwed up his eyes appreciatively.

'Straight from the fashion magazines! You must tell me some time what made you want to come to an isolated part of the world like this.' He took her arm as they went outside into hot clear sunshine. 'We'll have a look around the homestead area, Keitha. Unusual name, that. I hope I've got it right, Aunt Grace's writing's not the best. Ask any questions you want—I'm at your disposal.'

'Thank you,' said Keitha stiffly. She was not sure that she wanted him to call her by her first name, but to protest would be too stuffy. She wished though that he would leave go of her arm, for she found his touch unnerving. There was something so personal about it. He took her down a covered way that led to a huge kitchen, the domain of Mrs Dimmick, absent for the moment. The old-fashioned scrubbed deal table was spotlessly clean, as were the shining laminex counters. There was an immense fuel stove, a freezer and a refrigerator. On the verandah Lena and another aboriginal girl were peeling vegetables.

'The stockmen are away at mustering camp,' Dane told Keitha. 'They have a camp cook with them and every few days the book-keeper or I take out fresh supplies to them. Mrs Dimmick's husband looks after the vegetable garden and milks the cows and does odd jobs about the place. A very handy man is Harry ... Now out here we have the holding yards and the outbuildings.' He held a gate open and Keitha walked through and looked about her curiously, wishing that she had brought her sunglasses. She began to see why Dane Langley's eyes always seemed to be narrowed. He had let go of her arm now and walked a little way ahead of her, pointing out the various buildings and so on in a businesslike way.

'Poultry down there—can you hear a cackle? Means fresh eggs and chicken as a change from beef. Here's the stockmen's mess, next the meat house, and then we have the garage and work shop and store sheds ... Stockmen's quarters—most of them are aboriginals, wonderful riders, and good with the cattle. Down by those trees is Len Hooper's bungalow where he lives with his wife. He's my head stockman and my right arm.' He waited for a moment while she caught him up. The sun was hot on her arms and she was glad of her hat.

'Here we have the saddle shed and hay store. Feel like a walk over to the drafting yards and the dip? No?' His mocking look suddenly softened, and Keitha lowered her head so that the brim of her hat shielded her eyes from him.

Strong brown fingers reached down and encircled her wrist. 'You're drooping like a hothouse flower. Don't fret, pet, I'll lay off and we'll save the drafting yards for when there's some action there ... Better meet the book-keeper and get that over.' He let go her wrist as abruptly as he had taken hold of it. She found him rough, tough, unpredictable. He called her pet and honey, touched her bare arm, stared at her for minutes with those screwed up, fire blue eyes. She had never met anyone like him and she knew she ought to be able to tell him without a single spoken word that she didn't like his careless intimacy. But she couldn't.

She hastened along at his side back in the direction of the homestead, and his arm reached out casually and his hand rested lightly on her shoulder, bare in the sleeveless shirt. She drew away from him deliberately.

'I don't like to be touched, Mr Langley.'

'Dane,' he said. 'Christian names in the Gulf

Country.' His arm dropped to his side. 'Got a complex, have you? All right, I'll try to keep my hands off you. Though it's bound to happen again. I'm used to warmblooded easygoing girls—not city girls with their obsessions and maladjustments ... What kind of work did you do in England, honey?'

Honey. There it was again. You simply couldn't win.

'I was assistant to a television producer.'

He laughed briefly. 'Great heavens! You've certainly changed your stamping grounds! How the other half lives, eh? Well don't be disappointed if you don't fit in—or if we're not as amusing as you hoped. We're just ordinary normal human beings, you know.'

'And so am I,' retorted Keitha. 'Even if I do work in television.'

He grinned slightly at that. 'Fair enough. But by the way, don't expect to impress the book-keeper. He's something of a misogynist—probably left a disastrous love affair behind him when he came outback. Right now, he just isn't kindly inclined towards even the nicest of girls, and in fact he's a bit of a hermit altogether.'

They had reached the book-keeper's office by now. It occupied one end of the building that held the stores, and Bill Sutton came towards the door to meet them. His eyes appraised Keitha with a hardness and coldness she found disconcerting as Dane made the introductions—very briefly and with no reference to the reason for Keitha's being on Wayaway. 'He's going to have me off the place in a week,' thought Keitha, and was more determined than ever that she would not go.

The book-keeper was round about thirty, but his smoky grey eyes were a lot older, the whites slightly reddened. He wore an open-necked shirt and shorts, and while they talked his glance went now and again to Keitha with a detachment she found chilling. She wondered if it was true he had left a disastrous love affair behind him, and felt a little sorry for him.

'Well,' said Dane after a minute or two, 'Keitha and I are doing a tour of the homestead area, so we'd better get on with it. The next few days she'll be coming round the run with me.'

Keitha looked at him in surprise, but he was shepherding her towards the door. She gave the bookkeeper a quick and friendly smile. 'See you later.'

He made no response and she felt dampened. She wondered if Dane had noticed and almost expected him to say, 'I told you not to hope to make an impression.' Instead, he asked, 'I suppose you don't ride?'

'I do a little,' said Keitha cautiously. She had loved riding on her uncle's farm in Devon, but she was not going to make a fool of herself by pretending to be any sort of an expert.

'That's something—puts us one step ahead,' said Dane.

They continued on past the homestead garden and through a thick belt of trees to the flat that sloped gently down to the lagoon.

It was an immense sheet of water, bluer than the clear sky above. Tall gum trees and smaller eucalypts, white tea trees and a variety of acacias were grouped along the banks. Patches of lotus lilies spread across the water here and there, their pink and white flowers very beautiful against the bright broad leaves. With a whirr of wings a swarm of brightly coloured little birds flew up from the tall grass to settle further along the flat.

'Painted finches,' said Dane, his eyes following their flight. 'Pretty things, aren't they? Come down here at sundown if you're interested in bird life, Keitha—

you'll see plenty of it. Kate observes patiently and eternally, and is for ever doing sketches that she develops into line and wash drawings. You might like them. Kate is very creative and has a great reverence for nature. Get her to show you some of her work—she takes it so much for granted she's not likely to think it could be of much interest to anyone. It will show you another aspect of the outback people,' he added dryly, leaning back against the smooth white trunk of a tree. 'We still make our own amusements here to a large extent ... Well, you've been very quiet. Any questions?'

'Yes. I'd like to know why you're so sure I'm not the right person to work for Mrs Drummond.'

He quirked an eyebrow at her. 'You don't answer the requirements I laid out in writing for my aunt.'

'Mrs Warner must have thought I did,' she persisted —though she knew that was not true. 'Besides, it's not a job that requires any special training, is it?'

'That's true enough. But some strength of will— some force of personality—are necessary. Do you think you can put your twenty or so years against a woman roughly twice your age? I doubt it, determined though you might be. Patty's been coming over to Wayaway far too often—encroaching on our lives, on Kate's preserves. Kate is a highly organised person and likes to run things her own way, and to be free to use the leisure she creates for her painting.'

'Then that's why I must go round the run with you,' said Keitha thoughtfully.

'A nice piece of deduction, honey, but wrong. You'll come around the run with me because as your host it's up to me to see you get something worthwhile out of your visit to Wayaway.'

'I don't care for your use of the word visit. And if all I must do is see that Mrs Drummond is happy and occupied at the outstation, I don't think it will be so difficult. I get on with *most* people,' she added, giving him a dark look. 'Rather than waste your time, wouldn't it be a good idea if I were to go straight to the outstation and settle in there?'

'Honey,' he drawled, 'I can't let you go over there and shack up with the overseer. That's not to be considered at all.' Keitha flushed at the phrase and bit her lip. 'No, you'll do as I say and come around with me. That way you'll get a good look at this particular part of sunny Queensland before you take off.'

So he remembered what she had said on the island— and he was holding it against her, imagining, no doubt, that she had no intention of staying here any more than a week or two in any case. Well, she would stay six months if it suited her. Meanwhile—right! She would go out on the run with the boss. That would suit her very well. She glanced up and met his eyes.

'You're altogether too kind, Mr Langley.'

'I'm your host,' he said blandly. 'And I wish you'd try and call me Dane.'

CHAPTER THREE

KEITHA slept soundly that night. She had no dreams at all. When she woke it was well and truly daylight and she padded out on to the verandah on her bare feet to look at the morning. There was little of the vast plain visible through the thick sheltering screen of mango trees and oleanders that crowded around the house, keeping it cool and protecting it from the glare. Down towards the lagoon lay the vegetable garden, and she could see the dark shining leaves and bright globes of fruit on the citrus trees.

She dressed quickly in shirt and jeans and tied her bronze-brown hair back securely. She used only the most basic make-up—cream, and powder to protect her skin from the sun and the dust. No eye make-up at all. It didn't look right in this stark primitive setting. Even at the coast she had used it sparingly, for the bright sunshine emphasised anything that smacked of the artificial. Her lashes were naturally thick and dark, and her eyes this morning looked bright and sparkling and full of health.

Early though it was, she found when she went out to breakfast on the side verandah that Dane had gone out to the mustering camp long ago, and she felt a pang of disappointment. She refused steak and eggs and ate the grapefruit and toast that Lena brought her and drank two cups of coffee. Kate was busy issuing the orders for the day and seeing that the house girls got on with their work. The book-keeper, who ate with the family, was nowhere to be seen, so Keitha breakfasted alone.

Afterwards, she tidied her room and fetched her hat,

for she had decided to go down to the store and talk to Bill Sutton. She was not going to let his attitude frighten her away. Perhaps if she asked him, he might take her out riding. But as she walked around the verandah she came face to face with Dane Langley.

His eyes checked her over efficiently.

'Very nice! I guess a girl like you has something for every occasion in her wardrobe. What are we going to do with you today?'

'You don't need to do anything with me,' said Keitha with a bright smile. 'I can ride, you know, and I don't want to put you out. If I have your permission to saddle up one of the horses, then I can go around the run myself.'

'You'd be lost inside of five minutes,' he said dryly.

'I don't think so. But if you're worried, then I shall ask Bill Sutton to take me out.'

His eyes glinted dangerously. 'I've warned you about that. You'll find yourself out of luck. Apart from the fact that the book-keeper has plenty to keep him busy, he's just not interested in girls like you, honey— over-civilised, over-dressed, and intent on nothing but fun. He'd have stuck to the city if that was what he wanted.'

Keitha felt her temper rise. 'Is that how you sum me up?' she demanded.

'Now calm down!' He actually sounded surprised. 'Don't take it so hard. I didn't mean to hurt your feelings. What's wrong with being over-civilised and up to the minute in your dress? Isn't it a condition of smart city living? And you're young and on holiday, so of course you're bent on having fun.'

'I am not on holiday,' Keitha snapped. 'I came here to work.'

'Well, we've gone into that,' he said affably. 'All the same, give Bill a miss. I have yet to see the girl he'll be

42

bothered with. And if you will go chasing after him, then you mustn't blame me if your feelings get hurt, and you do seem to me to be on the touchy side.' He paused and studied her intently. 'On second thoughts, I'll make that an order. Stay away from the book-keeper. A lot of damage can be done in a week and Bill's not madly happy here as it is. Our community is too small and enclosed to risk dangerous involvements, and it's part of my job to keep things running smoothly. In the outback, you learn to think long and hard before you get too personally mixed up with your daily companions.'

Keitha eyed him but said nothing. She didn't know who he was trying to protect—her or the book-keeper. But she had no intention of taking orders from him. He was not her employer. She would make her own friends and her own decisions. No matter what he advised, or what he ordered, if she wanted she would ask Bill Sutton to take her out riding.

'You'll come out with me, Keitha,' he said into her thoughts.

She hesitated only a moment. She did want to see the cattle run, so why not make use of the boss? Besides, Bill Sutton might not be free just now.

She went out to the yards with Dane.

He didn't take her out to the mustering camp that day, but she saw something of the run and she learned at least a little about it. She suspected that Dane was assessing her ability to ride, and she was on her mettle. The horse he had chosen for her—a little chestnut called Summer—was reliable and quiet, but not too quiet, and Keitha could manage her easily.

They rode out to one of the waterholes at a leisurely pace, talking very little. There, red and white Hereford cattle grazed beneath the trees or lay in the shade, and Dane dismounted and inspected the rails of a holding yard near by.

'Routine check,' he said when he returned. 'A rotten set of rails can lose a valuable mob of cattle and cost a lot of time.'

They didn't see a single solitary person in all the miles they rode, and once they had left the homestead area, they didn't go through another gate. Dane explained that there were holding yards at various strategic points all over the run—never far from a waterhole. These were used to hold the cattle temporarily before they were drafted for branding or for market, during mustering.

'What size is your property, Mr Langley?' Keitha asked, as they rode on through the shade of a belt of bloodwoods that grew on a small rise.

'Come now, can't you manage Dane?' He screwed up his eyes in the way that had become familiar to her. 'The Wayaway run's roughly four thousand square miles.'

Keitha stifled a gasp. Her gaze took in the yellow plain, a low gravel ridge, a thick line of trees that marked a waterhole or the river bed, the great flat endless horizon.

'Four thousand square miles! And all that land belongs to you?'

'No, honey. We lease it from the Government. Most of the grazing lands in the north are Government-owned. My grandfather took out the first lease here some seventy years ago, and the Langleys have carried on ever since. Most of the neighbouring runs are owned by companies, who put in managers. They're nearly all run on the open range system. That's to say, we have few fences if any. The waterholes keep the cattle from straying too far—they're all we need in the way of restraint, except in the Wet.'

'I should like to see the stockmen mustering,' said

44

Keitha after a few moments.

'So you shall. I'll take you out to the camp in a day or two.'

'What is this muster for?' she asked curiously, and he sent her an amused look.

'Want to make notes? Is it to go in a letter home? What family have you left behind in England, Keitha? Or are they all out here?'

What a barrage of questions! She answered the last couple.

'Only my brother is here. Back home I lived with the aunt who brought me up.'

'Isn't there a lover somewhere in the background?' he asked shrewdly.

The abrupt question took her by surprise and she coloured furiously. He was certainly determined to find out all he could about her! 'That's my own business!'

'So it is. But I calculated it wouldn't be solely on your aunt's account you were so dead against settling in Queensland.'

'I have a job to go back to,' she said, riding a little ahead of him.

'Oh yes—the television thing. Are you in love with your boss? Or is that too much of a cliché?'

Keitha didn't answer. She touched Summer's flanks with her heels and raced ahead, revelling in the sensation of flying over the ground. He joined her again in a patch of open forest where she rode more sedately, and took up their conversation at the point before which it had become personal.

'Ready to have your question about the muster answered?'

'It doesn't matter. I can find out anything I want to know later, if it's too much bother,' she said coolly.

'Honey, it's no bother. A cattleman is always ready

to talk about his fun. The problem is to stop us ...
The men are mustering to brand and earmark the
calves and cleanskins, to desex where it's necessary,
and to cull inferior cows. We're interested in improv-
ing herd quality on Wayaway, hence we muster most
of the year except during the Wet. We have a big area
to cover. Every two years I buy bulls from a stud
property on the east coast—that was one of the objects
of my recent visit by the way. Those are my herd
bulls—the ones we use as breeders. To make it work,
we have to stop the station bulls from breeding—hence
the constant need to brand and castrate.'

Keitha had been listening intently and with interest.

'A scrub bull, then, is one that has escaped muster?'

'Yes. I believe you're really interested! A scrub bull
is usually a wild 'un too, because he hasn't become
inured to the routine of yarding and drafting. In
rough country such as we have on the eastern half of
this run, over at the outstation, there are always a few
scrubbers however scrupulously we muster the timber
... Well, that's about enough instruction for today.'
He gave her a slant-eyed smile. 'I guess you didn't
come all this way just to hear a lot of dry facts.'

'No,' Keitha reminded him smartly. 'I came all this
way to work.' She smiled slightly and refrained from
admitting that she found his 'dry facts' endlessly fascinating.

That evening he took her down to the lagoon again.
It was just on sundown as they walked through the
garden with its warm, sense-stirring fragrances,
through the beautifully laid out vegetable garden and
the grove of lemon and orange and grapefruit trees,
and on to the lagoon flat. As they came through the
trees, Keitha saw that a flood of pure vibrating colour
seemed to have been washed over the entire sky—
flame red and dazzling low on the horizon, then soft-

ening through coral and rose to delicate lavender, and, high above, a limpid watery green. There was not even the vestige of a cloud to be seen.

The colours were reflected in the long still lagoon, and already the birds were flying in, floating down to the water like leaves, their reflections coming to meet them. Heavy-billed pelicans waded off shore, and then came the long-legged, long-billed ibises, a pair of brolgas, and flocks of finches, white cockatoos, and pearly grey galahs with rose-coloured breasts. The air was noisy with cries as the birds flew down to drink.

Keitha had never seen such a sight. She could have stood and watched for ever. The man beside her was silent. Once she was aware that his hand was reaching out to her, but it stopped in mid-air and fell back at his side, and she knew a fleeting regret.

They stayed there until the sky began to pale, the richness of colour to disperse. Then for some reason they both looked up and saw the first trembling white star prick like a crystal through the colourless gauze of the sky above. Dane said softly, 'If anyone insists on compensations for living in the outback, sundown's one of them.'

They both turned and walked slowly through the trees towards the gate that led into the garden.

'Do civilised girls demand compensations, honey?—even for a short stay on a cattle run? Or is the thought of returning to London enough to sustain you?' He drawled out his questions as he stood aside for her to go through the gate ahead of him, and she felt deep in her being that he was determined to get her to talk to him about herself. Why? Was it because he was so used to being the boss—the man to whom everyone looked, with four thousand square miles of cattle country under his command? Well, he had forgone the right to question her when he had said he would put her on the mail plane next week. So she merely gave him an enigmatic smile and hoped he found her as maddening as she found him.

There was no doubt that he had immense personal magnetism. At the homestead at night, she found that simply to be sitting in one of the cane chairs on the verandah near him was infinitely disturbing. She was acutely conscious of his presence all the time. He had a passion for Beethoven symphonies and after dinner would select one or two to play on the record player, then sit out on the verandah to listen. It was a routine, this sitting out on the verandah at night—smoking, listening to music, staring out over the garden at the immense star-studded sky and the limitless plains glimpsed through trees that were heavy with perfume. Sometimes Kate sat there too, though more often than not she was painting. Bill Sutton usually returned to his own quarters after dinner, so Keitha and Dane sat alone, while from the darkness of the homestead behind them music swelled, filling the great empty silence of the outback night. It was infinitely more moving than music heard in a London flat. The lovely sound seemed to invade Keitha's innermost being and there it wrought an almost chemical change that was awesome and frightening...

She went out on the run with Dane every day. He was always up before dawn to drive out to the mustering camp, but he came back to the homestead for her later on. She felt she must be an imposition, but Kate told her calmly that Dane would have done the same for any guest. He had a head stockman upon whom he could depend absolutely, and had he wished could have spent much of the year at the bungalow on the coast, or in his harbourside apartment in Sydney. Yet he kept his hands on the reins at Wayaway, and as a result it was one of the best cattle stations in the Gulf

48

Country. So Kate said.

Keitha liked Kate—even if she was entirely devoted to the boss of Wayaway and completely blind to the fact that he just might have the odd flaw in his make-up. In Kate's eyes he could do no wrong, and there was no problem that he could not solve.

Kate initiated Keitha into the mysteries of the station radio transceiver, located in the office in the homestead. Station routine demanded that someone—usually Kate—tune in three times a day, to the early morning, the midday, and the afternoon schedules. Keitha had the opportunity to listen only once, and then only to the first part of the broadcast, that included weather checks from various cattle stations, calls to the doctor, and incoming and outgoing telegrams. She knew that this was followed by the galah session, when all the news of the district was passed around.

One morning while she and Kate were having a cup of coffee on the verandah and she was waiting for Dane to take her out on the run, she asked idly, 'Does everyone know that I am at Wayaway, Kate?'

Kate gave her an odd look.

'Nobody seems to know. I sometimes wonder how you managed it on the plane.'

'I think I was identified with some American tourists,' said Keitha, and Kate's slight frown disappeared.

'That would explain it. No one's breathed a word about you on any of the scheds, and I did wonder.'

'Does Mary Creek come on the air?' Keitha wanted to know.

'Yes, of course. I was talking to Patty yesterday afternoon. Melanie is having a wonderful time with the boys over there.'

'Haven't you told *her* that I'm here?'

Kate looked at her almost apologetically. 'No, dear.

49

Dane doesn't want that. He wants Patty and Melanie to stay at Mary Creek a little longer. And after all, you're not to stay, are you?'

'So *Dane* says. But even if Mrs Drummond knew I was here, she would hardly cut short her holiday on that account, would she?'

Kate smiled faintly. 'Dane thinks she would. And I think so too.'

It didn't make sense to Keitha, but she said no more.

By now she had seen some of Kate's paintings which she did solely to amuse herself. They were all bird or plant studies—meticulous, detailed, delicate and true in colour and altogether delightful. Aunt Jane would love them, and Donn would find them so wildly old-fashioned he would long to have one to hang in his flat. Keitha determined to sound Kate out about a sale one day.

The book-keeper she encountered at dinner, but rarely otherwise. One morning she rose rather earlier than usual and having breakfasted made her way to the store on the excuse of needing an extra pair of jeans and a more serviceable hat than her red straw. Bill Sutton's uncompromising, 'What do you want?' when she knocked on his office door was disconcerting, but she smiled determinedly and told him without fuss. He didn't smile back—he had not smiled at her even once—but he unlocked the store and let her in ahead of him.

It was a long room with a wooden floor and a counter at one side. On the rows of shelves that reached from floor to ceiling was ranged an enormous variety of commodities—soap and toothpaste, sugar, flour, salt, tinned foods of all descriptions, clothing of a utilitarian type, some bolts of pretty cotton materials, boots, hats, belts. Hanging from the ceiling there were even saddles and bridles. Keitha began trying on hats at once, and the book-keeper put a pile of jeans on the counter.

'All this stuff!' she marvelled. 'It's incredible. Do you need all this at Wayaway?'

'What do you think? Our main order goes out only once a year. The big trucks have to go over to town and bring the stuff back before we're cut off by the Wet.'

Keitha laid aside the hat she had decided on and reached for the jeans, looking at the sizes. 'How long have you been here, Bill?' she asked casually.

'Going on for a year,' he said not very graciously. 'Like you, I came from the city—Brisbane, in my case. Think you'll be here that long?'

She raised her eyes and found his, hard and cynical, on her face. 'Why not? If I like it here—and I do.'

'Now I wonder why that is?' He removed the cigarette that hung from one corner of his mouth and tapped ash off it. 'Could it have something to do with the boss?' The grey eyes flicked her way for an instant. 'He'll play you along, if that's what you want, and pretty soon you'll be well and truly hooked. It happens to them all. But make a note of this, sweetheart—there'll be nothing in it for you. Got anyone waiting for you at the coast—or back in England?' He paused, but Keitha didn't answer. She didn't much like the way he was talking to her, but she couldn't help listening. She had a very, very definite idea that he didn't like Dane Langley much, and she wondered why not.

He drew on his cigarette again and shoved some of the jeans aside. 'You stay here long,' he told Keitha, 'and you'll have eyes for no one but Dane Langley. Eventually he's going to marry that red-headed piece from over at the outstation. That's my bet. She was born out here, and she belongs here.' He stared at her hard. 'Take a look in the mirror when you go inside—

look at that frail pale face of yours, those great dark dreamy eyes. You just don't belong. But like some others I could name, you won't see it, you'll think you're going to be the one.' He tossed his cigarette butt on the floor and ground it out with his heel.

Keitha was thinking of what he had said about the 'red-headed piece from the outstation'. Was that Melanie Drummond? And was it true that Dane would marry her? And who were these 'others', who thought they were going to be the one? She remembered suddenly the girl called Dusty.

'If you want to try those on,' the book-keeper said, 'better take them over to the homestead. You can settle up later ... Meanwhile, take it from me, the smart thing for you to do would be to get out before you've ruined your life.'

Keitha gathered up the jeans and gave him a level look. 'I don't need your advice, Bill. I'm in no danger of falling for your boss. I'll let you into a secret, for I can see no one's enlightened you. I'm here to work for Mrs Drummond when she comes back, not to swoon over Dane Langley.' Outside she heard the Land-Rover come in and pull up on the gravel and she was aware of a feeling of guilt—though she was not sure if it was over what she had told the book-keeper or what he had told her. He followed her out on to the verandah, slammed the door shut and disappeared into his office. Dane waited on the gravel for Keitha. He gave one look at the hat perched on her head and the garments draped over her arm and drawled, 'Where's the point in getting new gear, honey? You'll be back in the bright lights soon ... Or was it just an excuse for disobeying orders?'

She gave him an enigmatic look, and he put his hand on her arm.

'How did you go down with the book-keeper?'

'I learned a thing or two,' said Keitha carelessly. 'But not about myself.' She left him to make what he could of that!

That was the day Dane took her out to the mustering camp. They drove out, taking with them supplies to replenish the camp stock. Keitha found the day an absorbing experience. The activity at the camp excited her and sitting in the shade of a tree she watched the growing mob of cattle that the ringers were bringing in. There was dust everywhere, the ringers shouted to each other and to the cattle, and every one of them was an expert rider. They looked as if they were part of the horses which they rode and, in fact, most of them seemed to walk awkwardly when they dismounted for smoko or for lunch.

She met Len Hooper, the head stockman, stringy and straight, with a face tanned to leather, and bright blue eyes that saw everything though they were even more screwed up than the boss's own. He asked no questions about Keitha, but he was not shy with her as the aboriginal stockmen were, barely able to bring themselves to look at her from under the wide brims of their dust-stained hats.

Driving back to the homestead with Dane, Keitha expressed her pleasure in the day, but she did not admit that the horseman she had enjoyed watching most of all had been the boss himself.

Dane said laconically, 'Oh, everyone likes to watch a muster—other people doing all the work. It's fine to sit in the shade of a tree and think what a picture it makes and what you'll write home about it all. But you'd really have something to enthuse about, honey, if you'd done some of the riding yourself.'

For a moment Keitha was at a loss for words. Was he throwing her a challenge? If so, then she was going to take it up. She remembered that other challenge of his—that he would in no time have her caring very much about his opinions. She didn't think he had won *that* yet! She said carelessly, 'I'd have liked to ride at the muster, but I didn't like to push myself forward, especially as this is the first time I've seen the procedure. But if I'd had a horse——'

He took her up mockingly. 'We'll go out again tomorrow and you can have a go at it.'

She blinked, but she didn't turn her head, knowing that he was watching for her reaction.

'Marvellous,' she said calmly. She hoped she had disconcerted him.

Later, when she thought what she had let herself in for, she felt more than a little apprehensive. She avoided Dane that night and went into the garden to walk restlessly by herself. She never had time these days to think about Donn, and at night she was always so physically tired she fell asleep almost as soon as she got into bed. Now, deliberately, she let her mind dwell on Donn, and wandered towards the lagoon. The sweet scent of the orange blossom, that bloomed on the trees among the fruit, made her long for Donn and his kisses and his loving words.

She was taken by surprise when she saw Bill Sutton strolling towards her from the trees on the lagoon flat. In the eeried brightness of starlight, he looked for a moment very much like Donn and her heart began to hammer when he passed her with nothing but a curt, 'Good evening.'

Now her reverie was broken. Her thoughts, almost against her will, drifted from Donn back to Wayaway and the immediate present. She went over that conversation she had had with Bill Sutton in the store and wondered at the vehemence with which he had warned her against Dane Langley. Had the girl *he* was in love with fallen under the boss's spell? And if so, who was

54

she? Keitha wondered if she would ever find out. His insistence that all the girls had eyes for no one but Dane had certainly had more than a touch of bitterness in it...

As soon as she woke the following morning she remembered that today she was to ride at the mustering camp. What would she have to do? She had a pretty fair idea that, rather than being expected to bring cattle in to the camp, she would be set to waiting on the edge of the mob that was ringing on camp, and going after any breakaways. She suspected, too, that Dane Langley would admit he had only been teasing her, and that of course she was not going to work at the muster!

When he came in to the homestead and found her ready to accompany him out to the camp, he gave her a rakish look from his narrowed eyes.

'Ready? Or are you going to chicken out of our little scheme for today?'

Keitha might have conceded if he had made the first move, but—chicken out! She had never in her life chickened out of anything—unless you could count not staying in England while Donn Gorsky changed his mind about the sort of arrangement he wanted with her in the future. At any rate, she was not chickening out now and she told Dane with a smile, 'Of course I'm not. Only I can't promise that my performance will even slightly resemble that of one of your ringers.'

'You'll be all right,' he said negligently. 'I've got a little black colt reserved for you—a great little camp horse. All you'll have to do is keep your wits about you and you won't take a fall.'

Those fire blue eyes were narrowed mockingly and Keitha's heart began to pound. If he wanted to frighten her with his talk of falls, then he was not going to succeed. She had watched the camp horses— watched them race after a beast that had broken away from the mob, shoulder it round, swerving at full gallop so that one of the rider's stirrups all but brushed the ground. She had marvelled at the way the stockmen kept their seat. Would this little black colt go through the same motions? And if it did—would she be able to hang on? She would just have to. Because she was sure Dane Langley was laughing at her and she was going to call his bluff. She could do it if she put her mind to it, and that she was going to demonstrate clearly.

He talked to her easily on the drive out to the camp. It took longer to cover the miles in country where there was no track to follow, and they had to go over stony ridges, across sandy creek beds, through trees and long grasses that might conceal a crippling stump. But the boss of Wayaway knew all the hazards, he was a more than competent driver and he never let his attention stray unless he knew he could afford it.

He talked, it seemed to Keitha, about anything other than the test ahead of her—because by now she regarded it as a test. If she passed, perhaps she would be allowed to stay. Whereas if she failed, would she then meekly pack her bags and go tomorrow? She was not at all sure. She only knew that to fail was unthinkable.

When they reached the muster, there was a sizeable mob already ringing on camp, and two or three stockmen riding round the outskirts to keep them under control. In the centre of the mob, in among the tossing horns that rose from a sea of swirling red dust, rode Len Hooper, drafting out the calves and the cleanskins. They would be yarded and branded and the rest of the cattle would be let go.

Dane had arranged for the black colt and his own big bay to be saddled ready. Today Keitha wore a hat with a chin strap—the one she had got from the station store—and she tilted it over her eyes as she stepped from the Land-Rover and looked at the mob of cattle. In a few more minutes, her heart in her mouth, she rode over to the surging cloud of dust to take up her position with the other ringers. She sat easily, listening to the bellowing of the bulls, the men's voices as they called out, the occasional crack of a stockwhip and the thundering of hooves as a few more beasts hunted from the scrub came to join the mob. She was so fascinated that for a little while she forgot that she was now meant to be part and parcel of it all until suddenly, close at hand, a bullock broke away and headed for the timber.

Her start of awareness was enough for the black colt which turned and went at a gallop across the flat. Keitha's heart was pounding and she clung to the pommel and put her trust in her mount. Dust was flying all around her and her eyes were smarting, but the next thing she knew, the bullock had surrendered and was lumbering back to the mob. It had been easy! She hadn't had to ride in close at all, and she was exultant.

She was breathing quickly and the perspiration was coursing down her back. On the outskirts of the mob, she waited again. The black colt fidgeted nervously and she knew it was on the alert. She glanced around quickly, wondering if Dane had seen her little escapade, and wondering if it would have impressed him at all. She had been lucky the bullock had been so easily dealt with. Some of the wild scrub bullocks would have been very different, and once they reached the timber, they were the very devil to bring back again.

All too soon, another opportunity came for the

camp horse to go into action. Keitha nearly lost her seat as it swung around and went flying across the ground after a great wild-looking beast. Surely a scrub bull, this! Keitha knew she was scared. They were getting close to the timber and still the bull refused to turn. The pony was closing in, soon it would be on the bull's flank and shouldering it around and then——

What would have happened then she was never to know, for suddenly Dane on his big bay cut in ahead of her, her own mount slowed and dropped back, and she watched, her heart thumping, as Dane swung the animal and brought him back.

Why had Dane let things go so far? She could have had a bad accident! He must be even harder and more ruthless than she imagined. It could even be he wanted to frighten her away from Wayaway. But she felt excited and oddly exhilarated, and pleased that she had stuck it out until he had forced her to give way. She knew that she would never have given in otherwise—no matter what had happened. She hoped he knew that now, and would apply it to other things...

She knew a feeling of regret when the cutting out was over, and the stockmen slid from their saddles and went over to the camp for lunch. Two of them remained to watch the calves and the cleanskins, and Keitha turned her horse and made for the camp. In a moment Dane was beside her and they ambled side by side in the direction of the camp fire. She was thirsty! Hungry too, and she looked eagerly at the hunks of meat and damper that the men were tucking into.

'For a city girl,' said Dane, riding close to her, 'you put on a pretty good show. You're no shirker. Tell me, honey—do you do all this for the sake of experience, or what is it that drives you?'

She wanted to say 'You, Dane Langley—you drive

me'. Instead, she simply smiled at him before she slid from her horse. Before she could take one step towards the camp, his hand was locked on her wrist. 'Better go down to the waterhole for a wash. You've a very dirty face.'

Did he think that would take the city girl down a peg? Keitha simply laughed and took his advice.

She tucked into the rough fare with great gusto later on, and afterwards rode on the flank of the mob that was being walked to the holding yard a mile or two away.

'I love it here,' she thought, taking herself by surprise. Donn would think she was off her head. As for Aunt Jane—she wouldn't be able to sleep at night if she knew what her niece had been up to today!

Dane spoilt the pleasant dream into which she had fallen by saying when they were back at the homestead yards, 'Well, you've one more morning left to you, honey. How do you want to put it in?'

She was somehow shocked. It seemed so callous. In her own mind she had won a battle, she had proved herself more than an over-dressed, over-civilised guest, and she was going to stay.

'One morning?' she repeated. Her winged eyebrows went up. 'I think I have more than that. When are you going to play fair and let Mrs Drummond know that I'm here?'

'I have no intention of giving Patty the good news,' he said dryly. 'You don't belong here.' His voice sharpened. 'Come on now, admit it. Your heart's back in London, isn't it?'

'I'm surprised to hear you talking of such elusive things as hearts,' she answered evasively.

'I'm as much concerned with hearts as most men. But I've been conditioned—by a number of things—to think of you as a tourist, someone passing through. I like to face facts as they are, and that in spite of your tricky persuasive way of doing whatever you set out to do and looking picturesque as you do it ... No, to-morrow we reach the end of a chapter.'

'Indeed we don't,' thought Keitha stubbornly. She waited while he called to one of the aboriginal boys to take care of the horses—he had left Len Hooper to bring the Rover back—then as they walked across the dusty yard towards the homestead she told him, 'I'm no tourist, and I'm afraid you'll have to re-do your thinking, Mr Langley.' That, of course, was no way to speak to the boss, and she saw him frown. Yet there was amusement in his eyes as he looked down at her.

'Is that meant to be an answer to my question? Are you telling me your heart's not back in London?' he asked insistently.

Was her heart back in London? Somehow she couldn't answer that question even to herself. Last night—strolling through the orange trees—she had thought of Donn with such longing. And then, distracted by the book-keeper and by her thoughts of the people she had met here in the Gulf Country, she had forgotten him again.

Suddenly she felt utterly confused. She simply didn't know where her heart was. She didn't even know *what* her heart was. A while back, riding at the muster, it had been very much here—right here, beating so hard in her body, harder than it had ever beaten before. That was the heart she thought of now ... She was at a loss and looked up at Dane without speaking.

He gave a sudden brief laugh. 'You don't know what you're asking for, Keitha. Patty Drummond will want to be rid of you even faster than I do.'

CHAPTER FOUR

SHE thought about that afterwards. So he wanted to be rid of her. But why? More definitely than ever she made up her mind that she was not going. But it was not because of Dane Langley—no matter what the book-keeper might imagine.

That night Len Hooper drove in from the camp, and after dinner he, Dane and Bill Sutton retired to the office. Keitha and Kate sat on the verandah engaged in the silent thought that seemed to come comfortably and without self-consciousness to the people of the outback. Presently Keitha asked, 'What is Mrs Drummond like, Kate? Do you think she and I would get on together?'

'Dane says not,' said Kate, unhesitatingly. Her utter and absolute faith in the boss of Wayaway was maddening to Keitha.

'I should like to find out for myself. Is that so unreasonable? I've come a long way!'

'It's for Dane to say,' Kate said simply. 'On a big cattle station someone has to be in command and make the decisions. I'm afraid I don't think you have any option, Keitha.' She looked at Keitha sorrowfully, and in sudden impatience the girl jumped to her feet.

'I think I'll take a walk in the garden and then turn in,' she told Kate.

She was coming in from her walk when suddenly Dane was beside her.

'Your last night,' he said laconically, looking down at her in the starlight. 'Pity, isn't it? I've got used to seeing you about the place. I've asked myself more than once what keeps you going. You're such a fragile

61

thing, like a bush orchid. And yet out at the mustering camp today you rode like a good 'un ... Well, no more to be said.'

She watched him warily. No more to be said. Perhaps not. But surely something to be done. If Kate had not been so rock-hard and inflexible in her support of the boss, Keitha would have got on the transceiver before this and told Patty Drummond that here she was and here she would stay until she and Melanie came back from Mary Creek. But now another plan was forming in her mind. She was not going to be put on that plane tomorrow. She was going to disappear. Dane would have to go out to the airstrip without her, because she simply would not be available.

And there was not a thing he would be able to do about it.

She disappeared most effectively the following morning, well before it was time for Dane to come in from the camp. She persuaded Mrs Dimmick to give her a lunch basket and a thermos and told Kate she was taking Summer out along the lagoon bank.

'Don't go far,' Kate warned unsuspectingly. 'Dane will want you back in good time for the plane.'

'Don't worry,' said Keitha ironically. 'Everything will be all right.'

They were going to be angry with her, she knew, but she didn't care. Of course she didn't go along the lagoon bank, but she chose her way carefully so that she would not be lost. She rode a few miles out in the direction of the camp, then crossed the plain to a waterhole where there were trees and shade. She had brought writing materials, and she would write letters to Aunt Jane and to Martin. Somehow she didn't feel like beginning another letter to Donn yet. She had written him one already—long and rather disjointed—

and it must now be reposing in the mail bag in the office. She was sure she would not be found. They would be expecting her at the homestead all the time, and in any case they wouldn't know where to look. She had made certain of that by telling Kate she would be by the lagoon ...

The time passed very slowly. It was hot and utterly silent except for the occasional screeching of cockatoos or the sounds of the cattle moving. Keitha didn't really enjoy herself at all. Ordinarily she would have been happy with her thoughts, but today she could not even concentrate on Donn. Simply because of a slight resemblance, Bill Sutton's face with its moody smoky eyes kept getting in the way. And then she was continually coming back to the question of Dane's possible reaction to her tactics. They were pretty impertinent tactics in one way, for after all, she had been a guest at Wayaway. But Dane was not giving her a fair deal. She wondered if there would be letters for her in the mailbag or if Martin would assume that she would be back at the coast this week.

She wandered down by the waterhole, and saw two kangaroos bounding through the trees. Otherwise there were only the birds and the cattle and Summer cropping the grass. She didn't dare ride around in case she was seen. She ate her lunch slowly at noon, and drank her thermos of tea. Not until at long long last she heard the mail plane droning across the sky did she feel safe. By then it was too late for Dane Langley to do anything about her presence on Wayaway, and with a sigh of relief she packed up her few things and prepared to ride back to the homestead. As Summer ambled along she thought with some trepidation of what lay ahead of her.

Well, she would have to face up to it, and the boss would have to make the best of it. He would see that in this battle of wills she had won. And after all, she had right on her side.

She did not feel nearly so sure of this when the station buildings came into sight.

She rode into the horse yard and left one of the aboriginal boys to take care of Summer, then rather slowly made her way to the homestead. The Land-Rover was pulled up outside the station store and Bill and Dane were unloading the freight. Neither of them took any notice of her as she slipped by, and she wondered if they had seen her.

Kate was on the verandah looking consideringly at an unfinished drawing and glanced up as Keitha came through the screen door, hot and perspiring and feeling very much in need of a cool refreshing shower.

'Did you get lost?' She asked the question dryly and Keitha started. She didn't want to answer that question.

'I hope no one was worried—and that Dane wasn't late going for the mail.'

'Dane is never late for the mail.' Kate sounded mildly reproving.

'I hope he didn't waste too much time looking for me.'

'No. He said if you were lost then you could stay lost a little longer.'

'Did he indeed?' thought Keitha with indignation. So the mail—the freight—were more important than she was, were they? Another thought struck her: Had he devised some other way of removing her from the station? She was going to meet that one head on.

'I suppose he'll see that I pick up the plane at a neighbouring station later on.'

She stood there, her hat swinging from her hand, watching Kate aggrievedly. And Kate held her drawing this way and that, put on her glasses and inspected it critically, and finally said, with her serene but enigmatic smile—only there was something disapproving in it now—'You'll be pleased to know you're to stay. If you'd waited this morning you'd have heard the news. Patty and Melanie are on their way home—they'll be here tonight. So Dane said that in the circumstances you may as well stay another week.'

'Oh.' Keitha felt deflated. Those long hot dreary hours by herself had been unnecessary. And Dane had let her sweat it out. Probably he had known very well that she wasn't lost—that she was simply making herself scarce. Somehow, she had to know exactly what he had done. She asked haltingly, 'Did anyone go along the lagoon looking for me?'

Kate looked at her in surprise. 'No. Why? Weren't you there?'

Keitha flushed. 'I changed my mind.'

'Well, don't be upset about it. You can count upon it—if Dane had wanted to find you he'd have done so.'

Keitha stood for a second and then went round by the verandah to her bedroom. She was fuming. The wonderful, all-knowing, all-powerful Dane Langley! Everything went his way. If he had wanted to, he'd have found her! *How?* She just didn't see how. And yet somewhere inside her, she had a suspicion that Kate was right. She had thought it was all too easy...

By the time she had showered and changed, Lena had brought afternoon tea and Dane, Kate and the book-keeper were sitting on the side verandah. No one commented on Keitha's failure to be at the homestead when it was time to go out to the airstrip. Dane smiled at her pleasantly, and his remark that she had a good colour in her cheeks made her flush deeply.

It was all anticlimax.

Kate went to the office for the afternoon schedule,

Bill returned to the store, and Keitha was left alone with Dane.

'Well, you'll have your wish tonight, Keitha. You'll be able to present yourself to Patty as her prospective helpmate.' There was laughter in his eyes and a tilt to the corners of his mouth.

'And you hope she'll turn me down,' Keitha flared.

His eyebrows rose and he gave her a long hard look, then got up and strolled across to look out into the garden.

'Well, you don't care what I hope, do you, honey? I'll tell you what will happen, though. Patty will find you too young and pretty by far to want you anywhere around this cattle run.'

'If she really needs some company, she may be prepared to put up with that,' Keitha said to his back. Her cheeks were bright with anger. Maybe she was spoiling for a fight.

He turned to face her again, leaning one hand nonchalantly on the rail. 'Patty thinks there's better company to be had at the homestead here.'

'But that interferes with Kate.'

'I didn't know you had Kate's interests so much at heart. It didn't seem so today when you did your little disappearing act. She was very upset.'

'Why? Because she thought you would fly into a rage when your wishes were thwarted?'

He looked at her in silence, but he was unperturbed, even faintly amused. 'I'd not have blamed Kate. Besides, when have you ever seen me fly into a rage?'

She shrugged and said stubbornly, 'Then why was Kate upset?'

'She thought you'd lost yourself.'

'And didn't you think so?'

He allowed himself a deeper smile. 'I had an idea what you were up to, honey.' He came across to her

66

and his hand rested for a second on the silkiness of her hair. 'You like to win your battles, don't you? ... By the way, no mail for you today. That brother of yours must have been expecting you back. We must talk about it some day.'

And then he was gone.

The Drummonds arrived an hour or so after dinner. Bill had disappeared as usual, and Keitha, Dane and Kate were in their usual chairs at the end of the verandah when car lights swept through the darkness of the plain beyond the homestead garden. Kate got up at once.

'I'll make some tea. They'll need it after that long drive.' She went unhurriedly towards the kitchen. The kitchen girls were off duty at night, and Mrs Dimmick, who with her husband had quarters near the kitchen, was never disturbed after dinner. Dane got up too, and going inside switched off the record player.

By that time the car lights had come in close, and now they swung round in an arc over the gravel beyond the garden. Dane reappeared and without a word or a look in Keitha's direction went down the steps. Keitha thought she had better keep out of the way until the greetings were over and the news of her presence had been broken. She listened to the voices outside in the warm night and strained her ears as if by catching the timbre of a voice she could prepare herself for what sort of a woman she had to impress. She knew practically nothing about Patty Drummond, beyond the fact that she had been widowed not so very long ago, and that her husband Bruce had been a distant relative of the Langleys. This much she had learned from Kate, who was loth to talk about anyone —except of course Dane, who was the apple of her eye.

As for Melanie—she was eighteen and red-haired!

The two voices that Keitha could hear were very different from each other. The young voice, Melanie's, was drawling like Dane's and came in excited bursts. The other voice was pretty and soft and reminded Keitha of Mrs Warner.

In a few moments the three figures appeared in the light that fell from the verandah. Dane had switched on the centre light to illuminate the steps, but Keitha still sat in semi-darkness. She saw a slight pretty woman with a brown face and black hair that looked untouched by grey, and a big well-built girl whose straight reddish hair was tied in a bunch at each side of her face. The girl had good eyes, a straight narrow nose, and full lips. She was a beautiful big country girl, and she looked overflowing with health and vigour. No one could have called *her* a bush orchid!

Mrs Drummond was quite different.

'I have such a headache, Dane. Has Kate got my room ready? I shall have to go to bed straight away. Mellie can tell you all about the exciting time we had. Those Palmer boys made such a fuss of her I thought it was high time I brought her home before her head was completely turned ... Oh, it's really wonderful to be home again!'

The voice babbled on prettily as they went inside, Dane's arm affectionately around the shoulders of the big beautiful Mellie. Keitha thought, 'Home again'. Did Patty Drummond mean Wayaway homestead or simply the Wayaway cattle run? Wasn't her home fifty miles away? And Dane, with his arm around Melanie —Keitha was irritated by the sense of hostility that gave her. But Bill had said that eventually Dane would marry Mellie. Yet how would he know?

She sat alone on the verandah feeling very much an outsider and a little forlorn. Inside, Kate's voice had joined those of the others, and she knew that tea had been brought in. She began to wonder if she should go and present herself when Dane came to the door and glanced along towards her.

'Come along in, Keitha. All the welcoming's over and it's time for you to be introduced.'

She got up from the chair aware that her heart was beating too fast. She had to make a good impression on Patty Drummond. Yet now that the moment had come, she was smitten with doubts about herself. Suddenly she knew that she should be a stout, dowdy, middle-aged woman if she was to inspire Patty Drummond with confidence. She was quite wrong. Dane had come along the verandah and now stood looking down at her, an amused expression in his eyes, his lips curving in a half-smile.

'Are you having doubts, honey, now that you've got what you wanted? Or is it the thought of those fifty miles?' His fingers had closed compellingly around her wrist, and she shook them off, tossing her head, and stalked ahead of him to the door.

When she stepped into the sitting room, Kate was pouring tea at the side table, Melanie was sprawling in a chair, her legs in their denim pants stretched out in front of her, and Patty Drummond leaned back exhaustedly in an armchair. Her blink of surprise when Keitha appeared was impossible to miss, and the girl made an immense effort to give her an easy, reassuring smile. Dane was close behind her and his hand rested lightly on her shoulder as he said drawlingly, 'Patty—Melanie—this is Keitha Godwin. Keitha—Mrs Drummond and Melanie, from the outstation.'

Patty's eyes hardened and red colour stained Melanie's cheeks. They had both straightened up somewhat, and her own friendly smile was met by blank surprise and even hostility, which unnerved her. Kate turned from the tea tray.

69

'Will you have some tea, Keitha?'

'Yes, please, Kate.'

'Sit down, honey,' said Dane, guiding her to the settee. He then proceeded to elucidate the situation.

'Patty, while I was over at the coast, I went to the bungalow for a couple of days. Grace was there, as no doubt you know, and I asked her to find a nice reliable woman who would be prepared to go out to the outstation and keep you company and cheer you up when things get too much for you.' He crossed over to Kate and helped hand out the cups of tea. 'Grace came up with an answer that was rather unexpected.'

The expression on Patty Drummond's face might have amused Keitha had the circumstances been otherwise. She looked positively stunned. She stared at Keitha as if she were a woman from outer space, and seemed totally incapable of speech. Keitha's spirits plummeted, and she caught herself looking to Dane as if for help. He waited until Kate was seated, then took a chair himself and screwing up his eyes looked around at the company.

Mellie spilt her tea in her saucer and coloured again, and Mrs Drummond at last managed a little laugh.

'Grace is a dear, but she's hopeless! I wish you'd told me what you had in mind, Dane, because I wouldn't have allowed it for a moment—things are not as bad as that! How long has Miss—Godwin— been here? You should have let me know!'

'Keitha's been with us a week, and I left you in happy ignorance so that you could finish your holiday and reap the full benefit of the change.'

'And so I have, Dane,' Patty Drummond said. "I feel wonderful—except for this headache.' Her brown eyes looked at him reproachfully. 'You shouldn't have done this, Dane—it's totally unnecessary, and I'm not a bit pleased.'

'What a welcome,' thought Keitha wryly, sipping her tea. She had not realised that she was going to be such a complete surprise to her employer. Apparently Dane had acted without consulting her at all. She stole a glance at Kate, and just at that moment, Kate said firmly,

'Speaking as an interested observer, Patty, I'd say it was not unnecessary at all. You've been so restless lately you've had me worried. Another woman at the outstation will make all the difference to you.'

Patty ignored her and spoke to Dane. 'If you'd told me, I'd have come back at once.'

'And I could have left today,' thought Keitha.

'That's just what I didn't want. Besides, it's given Keitha an opportunity to look around the run and get the feel of the place. As it happens, we're in luck, for she's taken to it like a duck to water.' His eyes met Keitha's mockingly. 'For all I knew, Patty, the girl might have hated it here and decided to take off today.'

Now for the first time Patty Drummond gave Keitha a full and prolonged scrutiny from her beautiful moody eyes. 'I'm quite sure she wouldn't have done that,' she said dryly. 'Though as far as I'm concerned she might as well have done ... I'd like another cup of tea, Kate, and then I'm going to bed. My head aches so.'

That was all. Keitha was dismissed. Patty Drummond quite plainly was not going to discuss the situation further tonight. 'Well,' thought Keitha, trying to be fair, 'I expect she is tired, and Dane has not been very considerate in springing a surprise on her like this.' But why was she so decided about not wanting another woman at the outstation? What had Dane said?—'Patty's been coming over to Wayaway far too often—encroaching on our lives, on Kate's preserves.' Why did he want to put a stop to that? Was it simply on Kate's account? Was that the whole story? Keitha couldn't think so.

Patty was saying a general good night. Keitha thought, 'I've really had it this time. She's going to refuse point blank to have me.' Would it be any use putting up a fight to stay? And did she really *want* to stay? Apart from the fact that it would be annoying to have to go back to Martin and admit defeat—why did it matter to her so much that she should stay here? Perhaps she wanted to prove something to Wayaway's boss! Though it might be better sense to take herself off to Brisbane and find work there. She remembered the book-keeper's warning about the apparently fatal charm of Dane Langley, but told herself that had no significance for *her*.

She became aware that Melanie and Dane were talking. Mellie was asking about the bulls he had bought at the coast, and now she was saying, 'Where are they mustering at the outstation? I hope Col hasn't done the Big Scrub Waterhole yet—it's the most exciting of all.'

'Tomboy,' teased Dane. 'I'll have to tell Col to put one of the men off if you go at it as hard as you have been doing.'

'I love it,' said Mellie. 'And Col lets me do absolutely anything. It's terrific fun hunting the cattle out of the scrub and teaching them it's no use trying to go wild again. At Mary Creek I wasn't even allowed to ride any of the camp horses. Most of the time I had to sit around with Jen and Mrs Palmer while the boys had all the fun. It was rotten.' To Keitha, listening, she sounded as ingenuous as a schoolgirl. But after all, she was only eighteen. *Was* she the girl Dane would

72

eventually marry?

She rose quietly and took her cup over to the tea tray.

'I'll wash the cups, Kate. And then I think I'll go to bed.'

Dane sent her a mocking smile, and wished her sweet dreams. Mellie looked at her as vaguely and impersonally as if she had been a stranger passing by in the street and then returned to her conversation.

Keitha didn't have sweet dreams. She dreamed of Dane instead of Donn and her sleep was restless and troubled. She woke in the morning with the depressed feeling that she had made a mistake in insisting on staying on Wayaway. Dane knew that and was going to have the last laugh.

She jumped out of bed and began to dress quickly.

'Not if I can help it,' she thought with sudden determination. 'I'm not going to be beaten so easily.'

Dane had gone out on the run and Mrs Drummond was having breakfast in bed. Mellie, in riding trousers, a green shirt, and a man's wide-brimmed hat, was wandering off to the horse yards.

Keitha said to Kate matter-of-factly, 'I don't think Mrs Drummond is prepared to like me.'

'Then you must make her do so,' said Kate surprisingly. She was sharing a second cup of coffee with Keitha on the side verandah before going to the kitchen to get the day's business organised. 'Dane wants you to go over to the outstation with Patty and Mellie.'

Keitha blinked. So Dane wanted her to go to the outstation, did he? Was that maybe because otherwise she would have to stay at the homestead here for another week?

Kate had gone to the office to listen to the morning schedule when Patty Drummond finally came out on to the verandah. Mellie had long ago ridden off looking very much at home on a big chestnut horse, and by now Keitha's nerves were taut.

Without preliminaries, Patty Drummond sat down beside her, proceeded to file her long pretty nails and to tell Keitha where she stood.

'I'm sorry about this, Miss Godwin, but you'll have to make up your mind you're out of a job. Dane has misunderstood my needs. I suppose you know I lost my husband last year—he was related to the Langleys and manager at the outstation—and of course it's left a big gap in my life. But there's nothing at all a young girl like you can do about that. I'm far happier coming over here occasionally to the people I know and love. You're obviously quite out of your element here, aren't you?' She smiled brightly and glanced over Keitha's fine cotton dress of vibrant orange, her pretty white Italian sandals. Then, with a steady and penetrating glance from eyes that were the opposite to friendly, she asked deliberately, 'How on earth did you ever manage to insinuate yourself into this household?'

Keitha felt herself slowly crimsoning. The question was pretty close to insulting! But to admit it was no way to hang on to a job that was going to slip out of her fingers unless she was careful. She managed a smile.

'Please don't put it like that! I was looking for work, and my brother is a friend of the Warner girls. Mrs Warner thought it might be worth my while to try the position here, as I was interested.'

'I'm sure you were interested—and I'm sure *you* thought it would be worth your while. I suppose you met Dane at the coast.' She didn't wait for an admission or a denial—and Keitha didn't know if she could have given the latter without looking guilty—but continued rapidly, 'Well, I don't quite know *what* we're going to do with you. It's very vexing. Dane obviously feels obliged to give you a trial out of politeness to Grace. But poor Kate must be thoroughly tired of you.'

'I haven't bothered Kate,' said Keitha quickly. 'I've been out on the run with Dane most of the time.'

That was a mistake! The fine nostrils dilated and there was a furious expression on Patty Drummond's face as she filed away at a fingernail. It became rather clear that she did not welcome any competition for Dane's attention. And of course—*of course*, thought Keitha, as it all fell into place—she wanted the picked position, here at Wayaway homestead, for Mellie! That was certainly why she came to stay so often. Keitha made an effort to allay her fears.

'I'd really appreciate it if you would give me a trial, Mrs Drummond. I've been so looking forward to see-ing the outstation.'

'I don't intend going back to the outstation yet,' said the older woman petulantly. 'You can surely not ex-pect me to change my plans to suit your convenience. No, Mellie and I shall stay here for a while and I'll see what else can be arranged about you. Someone may be going over to the coast in which case we could arrange for you to be picked up somewhere. The book-keeper could drive you...'

But when Dane came in to lunch, he swiftly put an end to these projected manoeuvres.

'No, Patty,' he told her. 'My mind's made up. You need company on the spot. I've promised that the out-station will continue to be your home as long as you need it, and you have a right to be happy there. You shouldn't need to be continually uprooting yourself and Mellie and coming all the way over here to us.' He smiled kindly as he spoke, and he looked so genuinely and warmly concerned about Patty Drummond's hap-piness that Keitha had to remind herself that somehow or other he was working things to suit himself. For she

75

was quite certain that the boss of Wayaway always pleased himself—and usually managed to persuade others that he had their interests at heart.

Patty Drummond sighed and looked out into the garden wistfully. 'I appreciate your concern, of course. But someone's made a mistake this time.' Her glance wandered to Keitha who was eating her lunch and keeping quiet, while Mellie, who didn't seem very interested at all in what was going on, did the same. 'How can a girl like Miss Godwin—charming though I have no doubt she is—be of any help to an experienced countrywoman who takes her way of life for granted and is used to wheels turning smoothly?'

Dane reached for a mango and proceeded to deal with it expertly, slitting the flesh from the stone with a curved knife, then eating it from the skin with a spoon, having first, however, passed half of it across to Keitha with an oddly intimate lift of one eyebrow that did not go unnoticed.

'I've brushed Keitha up a little on outback life, Patty,' he said consolingly. 'But if you'd rather, then she can stay on with us some more and get further training from Kate, till you feel she's ready to face life with you.'

Keitha thought she would choke on her first mouthful of the delicious juicy fruit. What on earth had got into Dane Langley, sponsoring her cause like this? It seemed he was always intent on forcing his will on someone or other, and this time it was Patty's turn. He was certainly winning hands down. Patty looked exasperated and helpless, and Keitha felt a vague sympathy for her. She knew that she would have to give in.

She said irritably, 'Kate has quite enough to do already. No, Dane, if you insist, then of course I shall try to train Miss Godwin myself.' She looked at Keitha

76

with dislike. 'I'm sure at least that I shall be able to find plenty to keep her occupied.'

'Then we shall all be pleased,' said Dane, sending Keitha a wicked look. 'Because Keitha is dead keen on getting stuck into some work.' He seemed to be amused at the whole business and at everyone's discomfiture.

Patty Drummond's idea of staying on at Wayaway evidently did not meet with his approval, for a short while after lunch he told Keitha that she and the Drummonds were to leave for the outstation as soon as they were ready. Keitha packed her belongings and reflected that now the time had come for her to go, she was filled with regret. Mrs Drummond was not at all kindly disposed towards her, and she had really been happy at the homestead. She liked Kate and Dane was, all other things aside, at the very least stimulating.

She took her luggage out on to the verandah when she was ready. Surprisingly, Kate came and kissed her goodbye.

'You're always welcome to come and visit us when you have some free time,' she assured Keitha.

'Thank you, Kate, I shall certainly come.' If I can arrange transport, she added to herself. She had not yet asked Kate about the possibility of buying one or two of her paintings, and that would surely make a reasonable excuse for a visit—if Dane Langley should demand an excuse! He had told her, when he broke the news that she was to leave that afternoon, 'Remember—one of your main duties is to keep Patty happy at the outstation and stop her from racing over here at the drop of a hat. I know you have a strong will—you've proved that to me without a doubt—so I'll expect results!'

She slipped down to say goodbye to Bill Sutton, mostly out of politeness, and found him checking the water and the batteries in the Drummonds' station wagon.

'I'm off to the outstation,' she told him when he looked up at her with that chilling expression she had earned to expect from him.

'You'll be back.' He slammed down the hood. 'Fifty miles is nothing. Girls come from a lot further than that to get a chance to captivate the boss of Wayaway.'

'I discovered that on my way out here,' said Keitha. 'But I haven't joined the queue yet.'

'No?' He was looking at her thoughtfully. 'Who was it you met up with on your way out here?'

'We didn't actually meet up. It was a girl called Dusty, I think, at Tyrone Park.'

'Justine O'Boyle,' he said, a watchfulness in his grey eyes. 'What'd she say?'

'Oh, that she'd be over after the border muster. Something like that.'

'Very interesting. Well, you hang on till the border muster, Keitha, and then you come along too. Will you do that for me?'

Keitha looked at him curiously. 'Why should I do anything for you, Bill?'

He shrugged. 'Please yourself.'

Keitha relented. 'I'll come if I'm still on the property. Will that do?'

As she turned away, she almost collided with Dane, who took her arm and drew her into the shade of some mango trees.

'You're a trier, aren't you?' he remarked. 'I just wanted to remind you to leave me a forwarding address—in case you forget on your way out next week. Meanwhile, enjoy yourself if you're able. You've got what you wanted, haven't you?'

Keitha returned his stare unblinkingly. 'Yes, I've got

78

what I wanted, thank you.'

'Well, chew hard on it. It's all part of sunny Queensland.'

On that inconclusive note they parted.

CHAPTER FIVE

IT was sundown when they reached the outstation, bumping over the track across the yellow plain. Keitha felt some slight misgiving during the long journey. What on earth had she let herself in for this time? Martin would be sure his judgement of her was correct. And that judgement seemed to be shared by Dane Langley. She could feel Patty Drummond's antagonism towards her in her very silence, but nevertheless she was prepared to make the best of what she had opted for. She had no idea of Melanie's feelings. Mellie just didn't seem particularly interested in her, which was a pity, because she thought Melanie would be a nice girl if one got to know her.

She sat alone in the back seat and neither of the others addressed her at all, though now and again Patty made some remark to her daughter in a low tone. Now they were almost fifty miles from Wayaway. Fifty miles from Kate and Dane Langley. Keitha had no idea what to expect of the next week, but she hoped that, at the end of it, she would still be there. Dane had been right when he said she liked to win her battles.

When they arrived at the homestead all thoughts were driven out of her head. It was sundown and the sky was full of birds. They swarmed like leaves driven by the wind, filling the sky as they wheeled and screeched and settled—in the trees, in the long spiky straw-coloured grasses, in the shallow waters of the lagoon above which, on a long low ridge, the homestead was perched.

Climbing from the car, Keitha forgot everything else

in her pleasure in the scene. She was eager too to see the house, which was obviously different from Wayaway, for it was built up on high piles, so that its upper verandah looked out over treetops to the lagoon which provided the house and garden with water. Keitha took her own luggage and moved with the others towards the garden gate where they encountered a broad-shouldered, suntanned man of average height, wearing the narrow gabardine trousers and checked shirt that were so familiar in the outback.

'Hi, Col!' cried Melanie cheerily, and Patty Drummond said, 'I'm glad you're in, Colin. Were you expecting us?'

'Sure. I listened in on the transceiver yesterday and heard the news. Hoped you'd come home today.'

He smiled at Keitha in an enquiring way, and Patty said shortly, 'This is Miss Godwin, Colin. Miss Godwin, this is our overseer, Mr Andrews. Miss Godwin has come to help in the house,' she added.

Keitha noted that. She had suspected it would come to 'helping in the house'. She liked the look of the overseer at once. He had a good-humoured face and an easygoing manner, and his eyes were blue and honest and friendly.

'How're things at Wayaway? I must have a talk with Dane about what size mob he wants for the sales.'

'I can tell you about that, Col,' babbled Melanie as they all went inside.

The homestead was old, but it was comfortable and pleasant and airy. Upstairs the bedrooms and two bathrooms opened off a wide verandah that overlooked the lagoon. Downstairs were the office and a big living room with a cool green cement floor and cotton floor rugs. Green ferns in huge pots added a soft note, and mango and papaw trees and leafy vines clustered closely around the verandah so that the light was cool

81

and green and subdued. The kitchen was in a separate building connected to the house by a covered passage, as at Wayaway, but here there was no Mrs Dimmick. Mrs Drummond cooked for the homestead, and the aboriginal workers had their own quarters and their own cook.

Col Andrews undertook to show Keitha the ropes while Patty and Melanie went upstairs to unpack and to change. Patty had said casually, 'You might as well start straight in, Miss Godwin, and show us what sort of a job you can make of getting dinner.'

Though Keitha knew very well this was not what she had been engaged to do, she fell in with Mrs Drummond's wishes agreeably.

Col gave her some welcome help and advice, but it was not a chore. There was plenty of steak in the refrigerator, and there were plenty of fresh vegetables and fruit from the homestead garden that Col told her was looked after by an old aboriginal called Tucker.

Col was inclined to be apologetic about her having to get dinner her first night, but Keitha told him cheerfully that it was the way she liked it. She didn't want to sit around and be waited on.

'I had no idea you were coming,' he admitted. 'You'll be able to cope all right, though. Some of the aboriginal girls help in the house doing cleaning and laundry and kitchen work. They don't do any of the cooking, you'll have to manage that yourself. You'll soon get your bearings.' He looked as though he would like to ask her a few questions about herself but was too polite.

Keitha decided that the status quo suited her admirably. With definite work to be done, she had more of a chance of making a success of her job and pleasing Patty Drummond!

That night Patty went to bed early, and Melanie

messed around downstairs, playing snatches of melodies on the piano, or spinning round on the stool to listen to what Col was saying to Keitha as he answered her questions about the outstation. She did not join in the conversation and there was a curious listening look on her face. Keitha couldn't really make Melanie out. She decided she would have to reserve judgement until she knew her better. Perhaps Mellie was doing that too!

Outside in the warm dark of the night, the aboriginal stockmen were in from camp and could be heard singing and laughing along at their quarters. Fires burned against the blackness of the plains, and tiny bright sparks floated upwards. Keitha stood for a while on the downstairs verandah before she finally went up to her room. Mrs Drummond had told her she must get the overseer's breakfast for him in the morning, and that he started work soon after daybreak! Mrs Drummond, of course, didn't want breakfast till much later.

Keitha made her early start the next day, and it wasn't so long after Col had gone that Mellie came downstairs. She was dressed in black jeans and high-heeled boots, and wore a man's broad-brimmed hat on her head. She told Keitha after she had eaten, 'I'm going out on the run. I'll have lunch with the men.'

Keitha felt a spasm of envy. But there was plenty for her to do, she discovered. Patty Drummond issued orders all day. It looked as though she expected Keitha to take over the entire running of the household. Well, it would be good training for—something, Keitha supposed, and she was not going to complain. She might be a city girl, but she could pull her weight anywhere.

'Don't let the lubras put anything over on you— watch everything they do and let them know you're watching. They'd far sooner play than work,' Patty said. She lounged about in the shady verandah and later went outside to water her garden plants.

The days were all much the same—and very different from the days at the Wayaway homestead! Keitha liked the aboriginal girls who were full of a sense of fun, and liable to go into fits of giggles for no reason that she could see. She found time to go over to their quarters once or twice to see the little dark babies and play for a while with the older ones. Those of school age were sent to live on the mission station during the term time.

Keitha would have liked to saddle up one of the many horses and ride out to the waterhole that was being mustered, but she was given no time for that. About the only task that she was not expected to take over was that of listening in to the daily radio schedules. The transceiver was in the office downstairs, and while Col or Mellie took the early morning schedule, Patty dealt with the others. One afternoon she came out of the office just as Keitha, who had been down to the vegetable garden to see why Tucker had not sent any beans to the kitchen, came into the living room.

'Sit down, Miss Goodwin,' Patty said. 'I want to talk to you.' She was wearing a finely striped red and white dress that emphasised her youthful figure, and she looked very attractive as she arranged herself gracefully in a cane lounger. Not for the first time Keitha thought it was a pity she should be living such an isolated and lonely life. She should marry again. But who would she meet out here?

'Shall I make the tea first?' she asked.

'Tea can wait a few minutes.' Patty waited till Keitha was seated, then told her, 'I've been talking to Wayaway. They want to know how you are getting on here.'

'Dane wanted to know?'

'Dane deputised Kate to enquire,' said Patty chillingly.

'Of course. I understand.' Keitha flushed faintly. She had sounded so eager! 'What did you tell them?'

'What could I tell them? That you are being kept busy—— But I shall be quite frank with you, Miss Godwin. I can very well do without you. Of course while you are here you must earn the wages that Wayaway is paying you, but I want to remind you that the week is nearly over.' She paused as if expecting Keitha to say something.

'What do you mean?' Keitha asked at last.

'This is not your kind of work, is it? And it's not your kind of life.'

'I like the life very much,' said Keitha firmly. 'And I can manage the work.'

'In your fashion,' was the chilling response. 'But you're far too lax with the house girls. These days they're laughing and chattering all day long.'

'I'm sorry,' said Keitha thinking the criticism was not altogether just.

'You see, you were not born to this life. Now Mellie —Mellie was born on Wayaway and couldn't live anywhere else. She will make an ideal cattleman's wife.'

'And now we come to the point of this conversation,' thought Keitha. Patty Drummond still seemed to have the idea that Dane was the great attraction, and wanted to get rid of her on that acoount.

'Of course, it's a foregone conclusion that Dane and Mellie will marry. It's only because Mellie is so young that nothing has yet been said. She is only eighteen, you know, and Dane wants to give her time to settle down after her years away at boarding school in Brisbane. She misses her father terribly, and when he died she was so afraid that we would have to live at the coast. Dane wouldn't hear of it. Luckily we had a wonderfully competent head stockman in Colin Andrews. He was promoted to overseer and it's made it a very happy situation for all of us. I want to keep it that way.' She looked across at Keitha from under heavy lids.

'Of course you do,' said Keitha mildly. She stood up. 'I'll get the tea now.'

She went out to the kitchen. Tucker had brought in some beans and the kitchen girls, Mary and Pearlie, were already stringing them, and even if they were giggling together they were hard at it. Keitha didn't really see that there was any cause to complain. As she made the tea, she thought of all that Patty Drummond had said to her, and of those final words—'I want to keep it that way'. Meaning the happy situation. Why did she need to worry if Dane was going to marry Mellie—if he was just waiting for her to grow up? Big beautiful bouncing Mellie, who still had so much of the gaucheness and uncertainty of a schoolgirl about her!

That night after dinner, Keitha walked through the garden beyond the papaw trees and sat looking dreamily over the still waters of the lagoon. There was an awesomeness in the hugeness of the night out here. Behind her the lights from the homestead shone softly. Mellie was playing the piano rather badly and Patty Drummond was looking through a fashion book because she was planning a new dress for Mellie. One of the bedrooms upstairs was fitted out as a sewing room and in the camphor-wood box there were several dress lengths of beautiful expensive materials.

As Keitha sat there wrapped up in her thoughts, Colin Andrews came through the garden and stopped a few feet away from her. He was smoking a cigarette and the tip glowed red in the warm darkness.

'Hi, Keitha. Not asleep, are you?'

'Daydreaming,' she said with a laugh, pleased at the thought of company. She had felt comfortable right from the start with this honest straightforward Australian. 'That is, if one can daydream at night.'

'You can daydream any time you like. I do it when I'm rounding up cattle. Leads me into a bit of strife at times, I can tell you! Feel like a walk, or are you too lazy?'

She got up with alacrity. 'I'd love a walk. To tell the truth, I'm a bit afraid to walk too far by myself at night.'

'Then let me escort you.' As they left the garden and walked down from the ridge to the lagoon, she asked him lightly, 'What do you daydream about when you're rounding up the cattle, Colin?'

'The usual thing,' he said. 'Girls.'

She didn't know if he was teasing or not. He had a very Australian sense of humour and was a great one at leg-pulling.

'Any girl in particular?'

'You're not fishing for a compliment, are you?'

'I could be,' she joked.

'I'll make a deal with you. You tell me your day-dreams and I'll tell you mine. Just now, for instance——' His arm went lightly round her waist as he spoke, and he drew her gently towards him. They had stopped on the grassy margin of the lagoon in the deeper darkness of a river gum, and Keitha, looking up, could see the pale blur of his face above her, the lips curved in a smile, the white teeth glinting.

'You'll think you've made a poor bargain,' she said. 'My mind was occupied with the various people who live on this cattle run—I was sort of turning over the pages and looking at them all as if they were picture portraits.'

'And where did you linger the longest? I'll make a guess——'

'Now who's fishing for compliments?'

She saw the surprise plain on his face, then he laughed. 'I may be a conceited sort of bloke, but I'm up against some pretty stiff competition in this outfit. I have yet to meet the girl who'll drool over me when she can drool over the boss.'

'The boss?' Now they were both leaning against the broad trunk of the tree, his arm was still about her waist and her face still turned up to his. 'Why would I be drooling over the boss? From what I hear, there are too many girls at it already.'

'True. Oh, very true.'

'And who's going to win him?' She didn't know what made her ask, but now they had started talking about Dane she felt a kind of compulsion to go on.

'It's not a case of who's going to win him, my good girl—it's a case of who is he going to choose ... And my money's on Mellie.'

'Really?' Mellie certainly seemed to be first favourite hereabouts! She was going to ask him to elucidate, but there was no need. He was well away.

'The boss could have sent the Drummonds off the place after Bruce died, but he didn't. Guess why not? ... Mellie's just the girl for a cattleman—she loves riding and working the cattle, she can talk sense about the whole show, and she takes an intelligent interest in the business side of it. She has the constitution of an ox, and as well she's beautiful and wholesome and enduring.'

Keitha listened to him in surprise. Did he really sound as if he were more than a little in love with Mellie himself, or was she imagining it? She hazarded a guess.

'Is it Mellie you daydream about, Col?'

He laughed ruefully. 'I guess so. But believe me, they're only daydreams. I haven't a chance. There's a pecking order out here and the boss has first peck. And rightly so. Besides that, he's top of the popularity poll. There's a lot of girls going to stay single until he's married and then—wham! There'll be weddings all over the Gulf Country.'

'You mean,' said Keitha, not believing it, 'that other men will be content to be second best?'

He looked thoughtful. 'It's not exactly like that. Dane represents a sort of ideal, I guess. It's the thing for the girls to set their sights on him. But once a girl knows for sure she's out of the running, she accepts what's in her reach and I reckon is perfectly happy.'

'How do you know all this, Col?'

'Because I'm the brotherly type—girls confide in me. And I kiss 'em and comfort 'em—like this.'

His arms went around her and he had kissed her gently on the lips when there was a sound beyond the trees and Mellie was there.

'What on earth are you two doing?' She sounded cross. 'I've made a jug of fruit punch—from a recipe I got from Jen Palmer at Mary Creek. Are you coming in to sample it, or aren't you?' She was down beside them now and Col put out his free arm and gathered her in beside him.

'Sure we're coming to sample it! Aren't we, Keitha? Just so long as it's not a love potion you're offering us——'

'You don't need a love potion, by the look of you,' said Mellie, pulling away from him.

'Cut that out now, young Mellie. And don't go spreading rumours that aren't true. Keitha and I have been exchanging life stories and offering each other a consolation kiss.'

'Why does Keitha need a consolation kiss?' asked

Mellie suspiciously.

'Maybe because she thinks she's failed to fascinate the boss.'

'Not true, Mellie,' said Keitha lightly. 'I'm one girl who hasn't even tried!'

The boss let it be known through Kate over the transceiver the following morning that he would be at the outstation for dinner and would stay the night.

'Get Dolly to make up the bed and prepare the room for him,' Patty told Keitha. 'And I hope you've planned a suitable dinner for tonight.'

Keitha felt tensed up and excited. She had planned a special fried chicken dish—one that Donn particularly liked—and as an accompaniment there were to be jacket potatoes with sour cream and a simple side salad of lettuce and tomato with an Italian-style dressing. Now when she thought of it, it seemed a little pretentious. Would Dane Langley think she was trying to impress him—and in a way that did not only concern her work? Tomorrow was mail day, and that of course was why he was coming. He had told Keitha that she would not suit Patty Drummond, and he was right, though efficiency had nothing to do with it. As sure as could be, she was going to be packed off on that plane tomorrow, and this time it seemed there was nothing she could do about it . . .

When everything for dinner was under control, she went down to the lagoon to watch the birds coming in for their evening drink. This would probably be her very last chance to do that, and she found the thought unexpectedly depressing. She wanted to stay on the Wayaway cattle run more than she had ever wanted anything in her life. That was surprising. Did she want it more than she wanted Donn to ask her to marry him? Or did it seem like that simply because

England was so far away?

It was a beautiful sky tonight, the colours so pure and limpid that they seemed to flood her innermost being. There was a very deep spiritual value in watching the outback sunset. It gave one a sense of awe and wonder and uplift.

Among the birds that came in were four brolgas. They flew down to the lagoon clumsily, necks outstretched, long legs trailing as they landed. They were big birds, four or five feet tall, and they had an amusingly grave air about them as they paraded together, long necks arched, small grey wings folded neatly. Keitha hoped they might dance, but she had heard that mainly happened after rain, so she was not very hopeful. She stood watching them with deep interest, forgetting the galahs and cockatoos and parrots, and the myriad small birds, until their screeching and the beating of their wings as they rose into the air once more in hundreds startled her anew.

When the sky had paled, she went back to the homestead, thinking once more of Dane. She was in the kitchen putting the finishing touches to the dinner with the help of Mary and Pearlie, whose admiring glances at the pretty salad and the brown potatoes split ready to receive their dollop of cream made her want to laugh, when she heard the Land-Rover. Immediately her heart began to pound.

She heard his voice a few minutes later as she walked down the covered way to the living room. That voice—after less than a week—did very strange things to her. One hand went up to smooth the dark hair from her forehead. She hoped the heat of the kitchen hadn't put too much of a flush in her normally pale cheeks. She could feel the brightness of her eyes. What on earth was wrong with her? She was ready for battle, of course!—ready to assert herself, to get her own way.

But she was afraid it was going to be a losing battle this time.

A pink-shaded lamp shone from the table, and another soft lamp by the settee cast its light on Patty Drummond, half lying there and looking very attractive in an off-white pants suit. Mellie sprawled in a chair as usual, one hand idly pulling a fern to pieces. She was still in her jeans and a crumpled shirt. And Dane——

They all looked up as Keitha came in, a graceful slim girl with shining dark hair. She was bare-legged, her narrow feet encased in blue sandals, and she wore her favourite jewel colours—peacock blue and emerald green in a soft cotton print that had an exotic eastern look about it.

'Well, hello! You look thriving for a girl who's being bugged by her responsibilities.' It was Dane's drawling half amused voice. 'I hear you've been having some trouble managing the girls.'

Keitha blinked, met his eyes, and wished she hadn't. She had best stay away from those electric blue eyes that were always enigmatically screwed up, sunlight or not! If a man like that had asked her to be his mistress, she might have been helpless to refuse. With an effort she pulled herself together and took in what had said. She didn't want to make a liar of Patty Drummond, so she said with a careless smile, 'It hasn't worried me really ... Shall I serve dinner, Mrs Drummond?'

'It might be an idea. We're all waiting.' Patty sounded petulantly reproachful—as if, thought Keitha, dinner was late, which it was not at all.

'Very well.' As she went, she heard the reprimand in Patty Drummond's voice as she said irritably, 'I wish you'd change when you come in, Mellie. You don't do yourself justice. Go and get into something pretty and fresh—it's not as if you had no clothes——'

Mellie was in a yellow concoction that was very flattering to her figure when they sat down to dinner. Colin, unfolding his starched white table napkin, remarked, 'Mellie's looking particularly glamorous tonight.'

'She is indeed,' agreed Dane. The two men eyed Mellie, who widened her eyes and looked almost schoolgirlishly from one to the other.

Keitha took her seat and the girls brought in the dishes.

'Mmm—the cooking's good,' Dane remarked presently. 'I must congratulate you, Patty. You've trained those girls to within an inch of their lives. Keitha can't have done much harm so far.'

'I never let the girls do the cooking,' said Patty. And failed to add that it was Keitha who had cooked the dinner.

'Terrific,' pronounced Colin. 'Must be a special occasion to warrant fare like this.' He looked at Keitha, and she shrugged slightly. Patty had silently accepted credit for the dinner, so it was for her to explain the occasion. She helped herself to salad, and Patty changed the subject. She wondered what the Warner girls were up to over at the coast.

'Grace spoils those girls of hers. I often wish she'd married a cattleman instead of an architect. It's a much more wholesome life out here than the one they lead.'

'Oh, they're nice girls,' said Dane offhandedly. 'What did you think, Keitha?'

She blushed as he turned his gaze on her, and drew her deliberately into the conversation.

'Yes,' she agreed awkwardly. 'I liked them very much.'

'So you're a friend of the family, are you?' This was

93

Colin, and Keitha could not help thinking how much easier he was in his manner when the boss was there. Patty was inclined to treat him with a trace of patronage, but Dane treated him exactly as an equal.

'I thought you'd have found that out before, Col,' said Dane sardonically. 'I've been hearing about the long hours you and Keitha spend together down by the lagoon.'

Mellie flushed and reached for the salad bowl, and Dane added, exonerating her, 'I can always depend on Patty to pass on all the news.'

Keitha was furious. The long hours she spent with Col! That was rather more than mere exaggeration. She wondered what else Patty had told Dane to her disadvantage.

Zabaglione followed the chicken and was praised by the men, and then Keitha went to the kitchen to make the coffee. The others had installed themselves outside under the starry sky when she brought the tray.

Tonight there was a moon, a small slip of a moon that slid into the vastness of the sky like a golden arc. Col wandered off when he had finished his coffee and Dane called after him, 'I'll be with you later, Col.' He turned to Keitha. 'Now this bit of business that's brought me over here—— What do I do about you, Keitha Godwin?'

Keitha felt Patty looking at her hard and saw her pretty mouth curve unkindly. She almost expected to hear her demand that Dane send her back to the coast, but that was not the way things were done in the boss's kingdom. And after all, she had paved the way very nicely. She had told Dane that Keitha couldn't contend with the kitchen girls, insinuated that she was playing around with the overseer, and who knew what else? The result was pretty well a foregone conclusion.

Unconsciously she sighed. 'Well, what *do* you do

about me, Mr Langley?'

Suddenly she thought she saw the glint of laughter in his eyes. He put his cup aside, stood up and said gravely, 'I think we'd better go into the office. Will you excuse us, Patty?'

CHAPTER SIX

'So you think too much is expected of you, do you?' he asked two minutes later when she was sitting opposite him in the office.

'Not at all,' contradicted Keitha with spirit. 'I don't mind the work at all—I certainly didn't expect to be paid for sitting around doing nothing.'

He was watching her steadily, his eyes screwed up, that mobile mouth curved in an enigmatic smile. Keitha could not keep her eyes off him—the lines beside his eyes, the sunbleached hair that was a little too long and a little untidy, the jutting chin; and that mouth—— She lowered her lashes defensively to give herself a chance to regain her senses.

'The dinner tonight was superb,' he said after a moment. 'Who prepared it, Miss Godwin? For I'll swear it wasn't Patty Drummond.'

Miss Godwin! What had become of 'honey'? Or was this the boss's way of intimating that this was strictly a business interview?—though it was an odd one at that.

'I prepared it, Mr Langley.'

'You did, Mr Langley,'· he mocked. 'Well, there's a point in your favour. You can cook. I wouldn't mind a taste of your cooking over at Wayaway. Mrs Dimmick is a fine plain cook, and Kate, when she puts her mind to it, can turn out a hearty banquet. But you're in a class of your own ... What did you say you did in television?'

'I was a producer's assistant,' said Keitha. His praise was sweet, yet she felt uneasily that it was not altogether deserved. She too was a fairly plain cook, but it happened that there were one or two dishes that she had worked on to please Donn on the occasions when he had asked her to play hostess at his dinner parties.

'What do you do in your free time?—here, I mean.'

She nearly asked, 'What free time?' but said instead, 'I go down by the lagoon and watch the birds—talk to the women over at the stockmen's quarters——'

'And at night you seek out the overseer. Is that it?'

Her brows lifted. 'I haven't made a habit of it. Why? Is there any law against it?'

'No law. I just like to check up on what's going on.' He glanced at his hands, clasped before him on the desk. Tonight he wore a white shirt and a tie with his dark trousers, and his rakish good looks were very much underlined. She was watching him again, her eyes moving over his face slowly, when he looked up suddenly, disconcerting her.

'Are you ready to leave us yet?'

She flushed at the unexpected question. 'No. I'm quite happy.'

'For how long? When do you mean to go back to whatever—or whoever—you left behind you in London?'

'I have no immediate plans,' said Keitha. And she reflected that this was very true.

He laughed mockingly. 'You aren't very forthcoming. Too evasive by far ... I have a notion I'm asking for trouble if I don't chuck you out right away.' He pushed back his chair abruptly. 'All the same, we'll have another round ... By the way, have you reached any agreement with Patty about taking time off?'

She shook her head. 'There didn't seem any need,' she said frankly.

'Then I suggest a free day tomorrow.' He got up, signifying that the interview was at an end, and waited at the door for her to pass through. She felt dazed—incredulous. Her confusion was the only excuse she could find later for what she said then.

'Thank you, *Donn*.'

His eyebrows tilted and he looked displeased. 'The name's Dane, honey.'

She was scarlet and could have bitten out her tongue.

She didn't see him again till the following morning, for he left her then to find Colin. In the living room Mellie was messing about disconsolately with the piano and Patty was reading—or pretending to. She looked up frowningly when Keitha came in.

Keitha said cheerfully, 'Dane says I'm to stay.'

There was a second's silence—except that Mellie went on picking out a melancholy little tune in the treble.

'Oh? Then if that's what you want, I suppose you must think yourself very lucky,' said Patty. 'How do you manage to persuade people to let you have your own way, Miss Godwin?'

'I really wouldn't know,' said Keitha with truth.

In the morning at breakfast, Dane told Patty he thought Keitha had earned a day off. 'You've certainly been seeing to it that she earns her wages,' he added.

Patty frowned. 'I think Miss Godwin's been misleading you. I've been doing as much as she does and a lot more besides for many years now.' She went on quickly, 'I thought Mellie might go over to Wayaway with you today, Dane, and possibly stay a night or two.'

'I want Keitha to come with me,' he said implacably, and Keitha gave a little start of surprise and knew a feeling of pleasure. 'Besides, Mellie won't want to miss her day at the muster. How's it going, Mellie? Is Col teaching you to be a good stockman?'

'I *am* a good stockman, Dane,' protested Mellie. 'I'm just as good as some of *your* ringers, I can tell you.'

'I'll check up on that some time. Meanwhile, no showing off or taking idiotic chances. You hear me?'

'I hear you, Dane,' agreed Mellie. 'But I've been rid-ing all my life and——'

'Maybe you have, but you don't know everything, and don't you forget it.'

Patty came out to the Land-Rover when Dane and Keitha were leaving.

'I hope Miss Godwin will be home this evening, Dane. I shall need her in the morning.'

Dane gave a grin. 'Is she becoming so indispensable already? I'll send her back, Patty, never fear.' There was irony in his tone. Of course he knew that it was not because she was indispensable that Patty wanted her back. The simple fact was she couldn't bear the idea of her being over at the Wayaway homestead when Mellie wasn't there.

As they drove along the track out on the plain, Dane said, 'Kate's looking forward to a visit from you, honey. She's rather taken to the little English girl.'

'Has she? I'm flattered. I like Kate very much—even if she is rather too devoted to the boss,' she couldn't stop herself from adding.

He tossed her a glance. 'No doubt you're devoted to someone too. Tell me, honey—who do *you* put on a pedestal? I should really like to know.'

'Not you,' she said instantly, and he laughed heartily.

'I didn't think you did. You parried that question very nicely, Miss Godwin.' He didn't press it, but changed the subject. 'Here's a direction: don't spend so much of your time with Col Andrews when you're back at the outstation.'

'The rules are certainly very strict in the Gulf Coun-try,' remarked Keitha. 'I suppose it's no use assuring you I haven't spent much time at all with Colin.

99

Where, by the way, do I go for masculine company if I want it?'

He gave her a sharp look. '*Do* you want it? If so—to me,' he said with a glint in his eye.

Keitha managed a faint laugh and retorted acidly, 'Not for me! From what I hear, all the girls for miles around go to you if they have the chance, Dane. I don't intend to stand in a queue and wait my turn anywhere.'

'Well, it's up to you,' he agreed laconically. 'But there are times when it may be worthwhile to wait in a queue.'

'Perhaps. Still, I'm a very long way from the queue, aren't I?'

'Fifty miles?' He looked at her with amused surprise. 'Fifty miles is nothing, honey. A little matter of fifty miles isn't going to put anyone off—though there are those who think it an advantage to shorten it, and forget that sometimes distance lends enchantment. What do you think? Or do you incline to the view that distance puts things in their right perspective?'

It was odd that he should say just that. She thought of Donn, and wondered whether for him distance had lent enchantment, as she had hoped it would. She was beginning to suspect that for her it had not. She didn't think of him nearly so much these days as she had when she first left England. She said briefly, 'I haven't given it much thought.'

They drove on in silence for some distance. Keitha did not find the landscape monotonous, though there was certainly a sameness about it. Around the waterholes, cattle were always gathered or lying in the shade of trees. There was something mesmeric about it all— the stillness, the heat, the brilliant sunshine, and the huge all-embracing sky that grew almost colourless as the day wore on. She watched for birds and cattle—

and the occasional kangaroo that came loping through the trees or across the plain. She forgot the man beside her in her intense scrutiny of the Wayaway lands.

There was a rhythm here, a rhythm of distance and line, a feeling of harmony and meaningfulness. They moved slowly along the track. No racing along at fifty or sixty miles an hour here! It would take them two hours at the very least to reach Wayaway homestead. Two hours alone with Dane Langley. Keitha thought of the letter she had written to Donn—'My boss here is immensely attractive physically—one of those overwhelmingly magnetic personalities. You know? But as an individual he doesn't attract me at all. He's so assured, so wrapped up in his own world, so certain about the way life should proceed. And so very, very arrogant.' She and Donn had always talked to each other frankly about the people they met, but Keitha had never met anyone in the least like Dane Langley before, and she could not come to grips with her feelings for him at all. She wondered if what she had written to Donn was altogether true. As an individual, didn't Dane attract her at all? Weren't his self-assurance, his devotion to the world of Wayaway, even, perhaps, his arrogance, very necessary to a man in his position? Perhaps too his world was not so strictly limited as she was inclined to think. He had a bungalow north of Cairns, and an apartment in Sydney— and then again, she had known him for a matter of only a couple of weeks—excluding, of course, their first brief encounter on the coral island.

Two weeks! It seemed impossible. Perhaps that week she had spent going round the run with him had counted for far more than a week. Yes, she was sure that it had. They might not have exchanged so much in the way of personal confidences, but something had definitely developed between them. There was some sort of rapport. A crystal had been formed. She thought of that star that had pierced the sky one evening after sundown at Wayaway. And she remembered how Kate had said last mail day, 'If he had wanted you, he'd have found you.' Hadn't he then, really wanted to send her away?

She stole a glance at him, trusting that her sunglasses would shield her.

He acknowledged her glance at once. 'By the way, honey, I meant to remind you to bring along any mail you wanted sent. Or have you put it all in the out-station mailbag?'

'I have another letter in my handbag,' she admitted —it was the one to Donn. 'I put a couple in the mailbag as well.'

'You've been busy communicating, have you? Who do you write to? That aunt of yours in England? Your brother at the coast?'

'That's right,' said Keitha. 'You have a good memory.'

There was a pause. 'Another little matter I meant to bring up—that slip of the tongue last night. I object to being called by another man's name, and I had the distinct impression you called me Don. Am I right? Do you know someone called Don?'

'Donn Gorsky is my boss in London,' said Keitha, conscious that she had flushed. There was, after all, that letter in her handbag and she didn't imagine for a moment that he wouldn't look to see who it was addressed to if he wanted to. He would be quite open about it.

'Is? Or was?'

'If I go back, the job will be there.'

'*If* you go back? Is there some doubt about it, then? I thought it was quite decided. Or have you changed your mind somewhat since that day on the island?'

'Heavens!' said Keitha, her colour deepening. 'You're as bad as a four-year-old child with all your questions.'

'Some people have to be questioned before they'll give of themselves. In the outback we share freely—we don't have to tear the truth and the humanity out of each other with a barrage of questions. 'We're honest with each other. We know where we stand.'

'It sounds wonderful,' said Keitha sceptically. 'But I'm afraid I'm far from convinced. I haven't been here long, but I know already that everyone's wondering what *you* are up to. There seem to be a good many girls in your life—or on the fringe of it. But perhaps that's your way of sharing.'

He gave an amused grin. 'I didn't know you were so involved with local gossip. Do you listen in to the galah sessions?'

'No. I haven't been included in those.'

'We'll have to remedy that. Unless you're set on heading back to England. I don't think you really answered my question about that. Are you by any chance in love with your boss?'

For a second she imagined he was referring to himself and her thoughts whirled. Then she got her bearings again and parried the question lightly.

'Falling in love with the boss is a cliché. You told me that once yourself, and *you* should know.'

There was something exasperated in the short silence that followed. 'You're too elusive by half,' he said at last. He sounded displeased. 'Then will you at least tell me why you came so far from home?'

That was easy enough!

'I was suffering slightly from overwork,' she told him cheerfully, minimising the situation. 'I needed a break, and Martin—my brother—asked me to come and stay out here for a while. He seemed to think my

103

aunt needed the break as badly as I did,' she finished wryly.

'I see. And that's all you're going to tell me, is it?'

'What more do you want?'

'Oh, I want a great deal more. However, I see that I'm not going to get it just now. But I'll persevere. I generally succeeded in finding out anything I really want to know.'

Keitha could believe that. But she was far from ready to tell her life story to anybody, and was certainly not going to confess that the main reason for coming so far from home was to force Donn Gorsky either to forget her, or to forget his unconventional ideas about relationships between men and women! So far, he had shown no signs of forgetting her, yet she, distracted by a new and totally unfamiliar way of living, seemed at times in danger of forgetting him almost completely.

'On consideration,' said Dane, interrupting her thoughts, 'I think it might be a good idea if mail day brought you and me together each week. You can't have anything special to do on your day off, Kate will be pleased to see you, and you and I can get to know each other better. Does that appeal to you at all? Or would you rather we forgot it?'

He looked at her with that fiery intense glance, slowing the car almost to a halt, and waited for her answer. Truth to tell, the idea appealed to her very much and her heart was beating fast. But she forced herself to say coolly, 'You're the boss, Mr Langley!' and left him to make what he could of that.

Kate seemed genuinely pleased to see her when they reached the homestead, and over lunch Keitha mentioned that she would like to buy one or two of her paintings if they were for sale. Kate protested that they would be a gift, and promised to pick out some bird and plant studies very soon. Keitha felt she was pleased at her enthusiasm and found it a little sad that she should be so pleased. Had she no idea just how attractive her studies were?

It was a question she put to Dane when she went out to the airstrip with him to meet the mail plane.

'Doesn't Kate place *any* value on the work she does?'

He gave her an astonished look. 'That question strikes me as being singularly naïve. Painting is like breathing to Kate. It's as important as that—and as natural. I thought I told you long ago that she's a creative person.'

Long ago. Less than two weeks. Yet it *was* long ago. It was in another lifetime.

'You did,' said Keitha. 'But—other people—do they appreciate her work? Do they tell her how much they like it—how talented she is?'

'You want to be special, do you, honey?' he asked ironically. 'Don't fool yourself. Kate's pictures hang in living rooms and hallways and bedrooms all over the Gulf Country. Everyone wants to own a painting Kate has done. Christmas time she gives with abandon.'

Keitha felt chastened. Still, Kate *had* been pleased at her praise.

'Maybe we're not what you'd call a cultured lot,' said Dane. 'But we do appreciate what's our own. You'll find stockmen and fencers and drovers—yes, and cattlemen like me—quoting Henry Lawson and Banjo Paterson all over the place. Same way, we like what Kate does. But we don't protest too much about it. Kate knows what we think. And she's humble and unassuming, which is a good way to be when you've been given a talent and you're using it.'

They were almost at the airstrip now, and it was a thrill to Keitha to watch the plane coming down and to be actually in the station car as it raced in its cloud of dust over the track and pulled up alongside. The freight officer recognised her and greeted her cheerfully, and she peered into the aircraft to see who was aboard. It was as if she belonged, as if she were really part of the great outback. The freight was collected, and the little ceremony of the mailbags gone through. Later, as they drove back to the homestead, she asked Dane, 'By the way, did you get the message the day I arrived from a girl called Dusty?'

'Dusty?' He looked puzzled, then his brow cleared and he gave her a quizzical smile. 'I like that—Dusty. You must mean Justine O'Boyle. Yes, I believe I did get some sort of a message from her. Why? What do you know about it?'

'Nothing. I heard her talking to the pilot,' Keitha admitted. She remembered quite well what Dusty—*Justine*—had said about breaking through Dane Langley's impenetrable defences. 'Will she be coming to visit Wayaway?'

'Some time for sure—she's a regular visitor,' he said with a casualness that would surely not have pleased Justine had she heard it.

'What's the attraction?'

'What would you think?'

Keitha pretended to consider. 'The boss, I suppose,' she said finally. 'You tell me Bill Sutton gives no encouragement to anyone, so I imagine it must be you.'

'There's a trace of censure in your tone, Miss Godwin. Do you think I encourage her?'

'I wouldn't know really. I haven't seen you in action.'

'You know,' he said speculatively after the briefest of pauses, 'there is something amazingly ingenuous about you after all. To make a remark like that——'

She didn't know what he was talking about.

'Well, there's Mellie,' she said after a moment.

106

'You think I encourage Mellie?'

'Does she need your encouragement? You've known each other for a long long time——'

'So we have. I understand Mellie very well. She's a sweet girl.'

Keitha would have liked to ask, 'Is that all?' but could not go so far. Besides, they were back at the homestead now and the freight had to be unloaded and the mail sorted. She left him at the ramp in front of the store and went inside to find Kate and see what she could do to make herself useful.

They were talking together when Dane came in again. He had letters for Kate and letters for Keitha.

'I'll get someone to drive you back to the outstation when you've had a cup of tea,' he told Keitha abruptly. He stood looking down at her as she glanced eagerly at her letters. There was one from Aunt Jane, one from Martin and four from Donn—posted on by Martin from the coast. 'You'd better get home before dark.'

She didn't know if she was imagining it, but there seemed a coolness, a remoteness in his voice. She looked up and found his eyes watching her thoughtfully. 'Do you want to read all your letters now, or are you going to save some for later? You certainly have more than your share. Still, you're a long way from home.'

She smiled uneasily. Somehow his words sounded strange in her ears. She didn't really feel a long way from home ...

Dane disappeared, after saying he'd be in for tea shortly, and Kate went to the office for the afternoon schedule, so Keitha read her letters. She read Donn's first, and they were so distinctly love letters that they brought colour to her cheeks and for some reason exasperated her more than a little.

'I miss you with every breath I take,' she read. 'It's as

107

if my life has disintegrated. When are you coming back to London?'

One thing, however, he did not say in any of the four letters, and that was, 'Let's get married.' Yet he *knew* how she felt about the other thing. She sat still and thought about him, and sometimes Bill Sutton's image got in the way, and sometimes Dane Langley's did. She concentrated hard on Donn's idiosyncrasies— the things she had loved about him. The way he chewed his lower lip when he was thinking, the way he ran his fingers through his hair so that it stood on end; the way he gnawed his knuckles, and looked at her with his eyes fixed as though he didn't see her—that was when he was working madly on some new idea. Dane never looked at you as though he didn't see you, even if his eyes were narrowed to mere slits. Those eyes saw every bit of you. They burned into you like a tongue of flame ... Keitha folded the pages and put them back into the envelopes and opened her other letters. Martin was seeing a lot of Julie Warner. The others were going back to Brisbane, but Julie was coming to Townsville. She was going to take the job that Keitha had turned down. She was mad about opals, and it was apparent that Martin was mad about her.

'I hope your job's working out all right—Julie says it's sure to with her cousin Dane Langley there. She says quite likely nothing on earth will prise you away from the Gulf now.'

Keitha made a face. Did absolutely everyone have to fall in love with Dane Langley? It certainly looked like it. Thank goodness she hadn't slipped yet herself, but he was getting some sort of a hold on her mind. She would have to watch it! Well, at least Martin seemed happy about her being at Wayaway now.

Aunt Jane's letter was brisk but affectionate. This silly rushing off to work in the outback would surely cure Keitha once and for all of rushing into situations with her eyes shut. 'Cooking for a lot of hungry stockmen will be very hard work, I am sure. You will be only too glad to come back to civilisation. It would be sheer foolishness for you to go back to your old job, and in any case I hardly think it will be available. When you come back I shall help you to the best of my ability to get something that will not overtax you, you know that, dear. On the other hand if you would like to stay on with your brother I shall be very happy about that...' And so on. Aunt Jane had always been fussy and over-voluble, but Keitha was fond of her just the same.

Presently Kate came back from the office, afternoon tea was served, and though Dane joined them, Keitha had no further conversation alone with him. In no time at all she was on her way back to the outstation with one of the white stockmen, a very shy man who scarcely said a word to her all the way.

She felt oddly disappointed over her visit. Yet what had she expected of it? And was it Dane's habit to—chat a girl up, as he had surely done with her, and then simply drop her? Or hadn't he dropped her? Had he been caught up mentally in station affairs? She didn't know what had happened—or if anything had happened at all.

Patty Drummond seemed pleased to have her back. She was resting in the living room. The heat had given her a sick headache, she said, and she would be relieved to have Keitha take over again. It seemed an odd attitude to adopt when she had obviously done her best to see that her helper was sent off on today's mail plane. Keitha had to get stuck into the work as though she had never been away.

When Mellie came home, she seemed innocently pleased to see her, and enquired about Wayaway and

Kate as if they were an intimate part of her family.

That night, quite by chance, she found herself sitting alone in the dark with Col. Mellie, tired out from a day in the sun, had gone to bed, and Patty, still headachy, had retired even earlier.

'Enjoy your day?' asked Col.

'Not all that much,' admitted Keitha. 'It was good to see Kate again——'

'How about the boss?'

She shrugged. 'I don't know where I stand with him.'

'Nowhere,' said Col promptly. 'So don't go getting any ideas.'

'I'm not likely to do that,' said Keitha, nettled. 'Why is everyone so convinced I'm going to get what you call "ideas"? It may amaze you to learn that I'm not so bereft of admirers that I've had to come to the Gulf Country to find one. I'm far from having taken root out here. Anyone who can manage it may have Dane Langley and welcome as far as I'm concerned. The general opinion seems to be that it will be poor Mellie——'

Col grunted. 'I've lived here for over five years now. I've seen Mellie growing up, and I've seen Dane bringing her along. I know for a fact that he's never come near marrying any other girl. It's true he's a man who plays his cards pretty close to his chest, but he's got his eye on Mellie all right. This year now she's home from school is the crucial one. He's waiting to see how she shapes up.'

'It sounds pretty cold-blooded to me,' said Keitha. 'I shouldn't like to be in Mellie's position if what you say is true. Tell me, Col—how do *you* think Mellie shapes up? You see a lot of her out on the run, don't you?'

'She shapes up pretty well,' Col said.

After that they were both silent.

110

IF Keitha had thought she would now get a bad time from Patty Drummond she was wrong. Patty was agreeable, businesslike and appreciative of the fact that Keitha took many chores off her hands, leaving her free for her gardening. Also, she was busy now making clothes for Mellie who hadn't had much new since she left school and was ready to blossom out.

The days passed quickly enough. Mellie and Col went out on the run and Keitha and Patty were busy about the homestead most of the day. Sometimes Keitha went over to the aboriginals' quarters to talk to the women and admire their babies, and even to give advice on little ailments or matters of hygiene. Once or twice she looked throughtfully at the two motorbikes in the garage, wishing that she could ride. They were used, as at Wayaway too, for speedy checking of water-holes and holding yards, but most days at least one of them was there in the garage.

Every evening the stockmen came in from muster-ing, there was the smell of cooking, lights gleamed in the darkness, and there were sounds of laughter and singing. At the homestead, the Drummonds, Col and Keitha got on very well together. It often struck Keitha as odd that Col should be happy with the status quo, seeing that he was in love with Mellie. She wondered if he knew many other girls in the district and wished that she could listen to the voices on the galah session. But for some reason, Patty never invited her. It seemed a silent underlining of the fact that Keitha was an out-sider—didn't really belong and never would. Even though Wayaway frequently talked with the outstation, Patty rarely passed any news on.

All through the week, Keitha was looking forward to mail day when she would see Dane. He had practically promised her that. The thought stimulated her and made her restless too, for she could not make up her mind what her feelings towards the boss were. She certainly didn't intend to join his band of admirers—and she had learned a chastening lesson from him last time they met when she had more or less glowed under his attention and then, for no apparent reason, been pushed aside and treated with extreme casualness. This time she might give him a little of his own treatment—turn on the charm and, when he had warmed to it, turn it off again. Yes, she thought that would give her quite a deal of satisfaction. She was sure it was not the sort of thing the boss of Wayaway was used to!

Late in the week, Patty asked her into the sewing room upstairs to consult her about a dress she was planning for Mellie. She showed her the design she had roughed out and asked how Keitha thought it compared with London fashions.

'I suppose we are behind the times here,' said Patty, 'though not so much as we used to be. I have fashion magazines sent out in the mail, and I order dress materials from Brisbane, or buy them in Sydney if we go there with Dane during the Wet. Parties do crop up occasionally even outback, and I like Mellie to have something unusual and attractive. Now what do you think of this style—with Mellie in mind?'

They discussed the style at some length and Keitha suggested a minor alteration that seemed to please the older woman. Patty then produced two dress lengths from the camphor-wood chest, and asked Keitha's opinion as to which would suit Mellie best.

'Dane would probably prefer the blue,' Patty said. 'It's a colour men are inclined to favour, don't you think? I suppose the muted pink and mauve is more fashionable, but I think I shall have to make that up for myself. It wouldn't really do anything for Mellie's healthy beauty.' She smiled at Keitha. 'This must all be a little boring for you. You worked in the television world, didn't you, and I expect there's a fair bit of interest in dress there.'

'A fair bit,' Keitha agreed.

'And in men too? I mean, it must be a competitive field where men are concerned?'

Keitha, not sure what she was talking about, agreed vaguely that it was.

'You didn't come to Queensland because of an unhappy love affair?' The brown eyes watched her shrewdly while the slender hands were busy folding the dress fabrics.

'No,' said Keitha with a smile.

'I hardly thought so. You don't look like a girl with a broken heart, in spite of those soulful dark eyes. But I'll admit I can't fathom you. To exchange that world for this ... Though of course it's only temporary, isn't it?'

'Of course,' agreed Keitha smoothly. 'I'm sure you won't need me here once your nerves have settled down.'

Mrs Drummond grimaced. 'You think I'm neurotic, which I'm not. But there's a lot of adjusting needed when one is widowed. Dane has made too much fuss, though. But we were talking about you. Do tell me about your work in London and the people you mixed with.' Skilfully, she led the conversation so that before she knew it, Keitha was talking about Donn. It was natural enough as Donn had been the man she worked for.

'He sounds fascinating. And of course you fell in love with him?' Patty suggested with a vague smile.

She had begun to draft out her pattern as she listened to Keitha, and her attention to what she was doing gave the impression that she was not listening very closely. Keitha admitted cautiously that quite a few of the girls had been in love with Donn, who was so clever and good-looking. She herself had been extremely lucky to be chosen to work for him.

'Lucky? A charming girl like you?' Patty frowned over a measurement. 'I'm quite sure he must have fallen completely in love with you. Isn't that so?' She looked up and smiled in a friendly way.

'Oh, of course,' Keitha said laughingly. 'He was mad about me!' Somewhere inside her a voice asked how she could talk so superficially about her love affair. Yet she could, and did, and it amazed her.

'And what happened?'

'Nothing happened—except that I was ordered off work for a while by the doctor.'

'And when you go back you'll have your old job again? Or has someone else taken your place?'

'Only temporarily. Donn assures me he much prefers me to work for him. But of course I may not want the job.'

'I see. Well, it all sounds wonderfully interesting.' Patty changed the subject then, but she was extremely affable for the rest of the day.

Looking back later, Keitha was to see that conversation in a different light. At the time, it had seemed lighthearted and harmless, Patty had been politely interested, and she herself had enjoyed talking about Donn for a change. It had seemed for a while to bring her old life back into focus again...

When mail day came, Keitha asked Patty casually at breakfast, 'Any news from Wayaway over the early morning schedule?'

Patty looked at her in surprise. 'No. What were you expecting?'

Keitha shrugged, and tried to hide her disappointment. Patty watched her with a faint smile.

'You're anxious about your mail. Don't worry. One of the stockmen has taken our mailbag over, and you'll get *your* letters. Dane always sees that our mail is sent over and I'm sure they all know over there that you must be longing for news.'

All day Keitha felt nervy and restless wondering if Dane would come. It seemed pointless to have a day off under the circumstances. She planned pepper steak for dinner. It was one of her best dishes and it was possible that Dane would be at the outstation for dinner. He would enjoy her pepper steak, he was different from the stockmen who couldn't have cared less about fancy ways of serving up steak.

But Dane didn't come to dinner. He didn't come at all.

'You're restless, Keitha,' said Patty—she had taken lately to calling the girl by her first name in a more friendly way. Keitha had wandered out on to the verandah after dinner and then come back inside again. 'Don't worry—your letters will come.'

Keitha was not thinking of her letters. It was Dane she wanted to see and she was annoyed with herself because of it. Yet she couldn't seem to help herself. What had she planned for this meeting that had made it so important? To smile into his eyes through her lashes—to fascinate him absolutely—and then to walk off and show him that he didn't matter one jot to her! Was that what she wanted? She didn't know. She only knew she longed to see him. Maybe this was what happened to you in the outback—you became obsessed with whoever was available.

When she heard the sound of a motorbike her heart

began to beat fast, and she could have wept when one of the stockmen clumped heavily up on to the verandah.

'The boss said he was too busy to come over today,' she heard him telling Mrs Drummond, but by that time she was going blindly out into the darkness of the garden, where she could get over her disappointment, wipe away her tears of vexation, and come back able to pretend that nothing had happened to her heart.

Another ten minutes and Col came out to find her.

'Hey, Keitha—Patty says to come in and get your mail. What's up? Afraid you'll be disappointed? I promise you won't—there are two letters from your boy-friend.'

She gave him a sharp look. 'What on earth are you talking about, Col?'

'Oh, come on, Keitha, don't get on your high horse. Everyone's private life soon becomes public property in the outback.'

'Is that a fact? It seems to me you're a very nosey lot. At all events you don't know a thing about my private life. I just wish you'd mind your own business.'

'Heck, I sure have touched you off! Sorry, I didn't mean to tread on your toes. Not another word will I utter.'

Keitha stalked past him. She felt a little ashamed of her outburst. Col had meant no harm. Of course he had seen that it was Donn's name on the back of her letter, and he was only pulling her leg about it. She was just too touchy for words, that was all.

She took her letters upstairs, and in her room read through them impatiently. It looked as though Donn were implacable. He was going to hold out for ever—so sure that asking a girl to shack up with him was just as good as asking her to marry him. Well, she could hold out for ever too. And she was beginning to think that she didn't really care *what* Donn did any more—

116

or who he shacked up with, so long as it wasn't her. Certainly he wasn't proving to be very considerate—especially for a man who claimed to be so very much in love with her!

A few days later, Colin came in from the muster camp in time for the mid-morning radio broadcast. The little daughter of one of the stockmen, a girl of ten who was at the mission school, had been operated on for appendicitis, and Albert was anxious for news of her. Patty had been in the office for some minutes and Keitha had just come in from the garden. She had been idly picking up some of the frangipani blooms that had fallen and wishing aggrievedly that she had been asked in to the galah session. She would have liked to talk to Kate and perhaps arrange to go over and see her one day. It was only an excuse, of course. She was aware of that.

She saw Col go to the office door and stop frustrated when it would not open.

'Mrs Drummond, open the door, please!' he called, and in a second Patty did so, offering the excuse that the door must have stuck.

The little incident worried Keitha. *Had* the catch stuck, or had Patty locked the office door? And if she had, was it to keep Keitha out of the galah session? It seemed mean and petty to Keitha.

When Col came out again he told her cheerfully, flicking her cheek as he came up to where she now sat on the verandah, 'Peggy's doing fine. Albert will be a happy man. Hey, Keitha——' He turned back as he had been about to go down the steps, the wide-brimmed hat already back on his head, 'You don't look all that busy. Like to come out to the camp with me?'

Her pulses leaped. 'I'd love to!' She was feeling singularly stale and in need of diversion. 'But I don't know if Mrs Drummond will agree.'

'Sure she'll agree. She'll have finished her gossip session in a minute and we'll ask her.'

To Keitha's surprise, Patty seemed to think it a good idea.

'Yes, go along. I've been wondering what we could do with you to give you some time off. It's an excellent idea, Colin. I shall get on with my sewing and won't be in the least lonely. Will you have some lunch before you go?'

'No, thanks. Albert will be waiting for news of Peggy. We'll have something out there. Run along and hop into your jeans, Keitha, and get yourself a hat. I'll saddle up a horse for you.'

Feeling elated, Keitha hurried off to do as he told her and in no time she was riding with him out of the dusty yard and through the tall straw-coloured spear grass. They went through a grove of bloodwoods and ironbarks, and across a dry creek that had steep red banks. They rode around the highest rise she had seen on the property, though it was probably no more than fifty feet, and she remarked to Col that this was certainly rougher and wilder country than that in the vicinity of the home station.

'You're right. What's more, you've got to know it thoroughly if you're going to run the place properly. I reckon I know every waterhole and every patch of scrub where the cattle hide out. I learned the place from Bruce Drummond—he started here as a jackeroo when he was nineteen, and he knew it backwards. Mellie's going to be the same. It would take a pitch dark night or a blinding thunderstorm to bush Mellie. She's a girl in a million.'

Keitha wondered if Dane thought so too, or if he were still waiting in a cold-blooded calculating way to see how she 'shaped up'.

Not far from the muster camp they rode into some thick scrub where Col had caught sight of a few cattle. He spurred his horse and was off at a gallop, standing in the stirrups. Keitha was having a little trouble holding her mount back, and suddenly she thought, 'Why should I?' She dug in her heels and rose in the saddle, emulating Col. The excitement of that rather wild ride did a lot to release some of her pent-up emotions, and she was hot on Col's heels when the two of them finally emerged from the scrub with three cows and a couple of calves lumbering ahead of them.

Col turned back to Keitha with a grin.

'Those beasts are well trained. They're not bush cattle. We'd never have got scrubbers out into the open as easily—they're as cunning as they come.'

She laughed, for she had been thinking that if this was all the trouble scrub cattle gave, there was nothing to it.

Now the camp was in sight and a sizeable mob was being held by a couple of dark-faced easy-riding stockmen, one of whom was apparently Albert, for Col rode towards him waving cheerfully. Keitha, occupied in watching him receive the good news, started with surprise when a voice that was unmistakably Dane Langley's said from a few yards away, 'Hold it, Miss Godwin!'

Her heart began to thud as she saw him coming towards her on his big bay. She put up a hand to straighten her hat which had fallen askew in that race through the bush. Her cheeks were flushed and she was still panting a little and she knew a wild thrill of elation.

Over in the shade of some white-boled river gums, the camp cook was busy with dinner. A slow stream of cattle was coming in from various directions to join the mob, and beyond the dust they made smoke was rising. There was a smell of burning gum leaves. It was a picture that stayed clear and bright in Keitha's mind.

'Who brought you out here?' Dane asked a moment later. The question came abruptly and something in the tone of voice had the instant effect of damping her elation.

Her voice was very cool as she replied, 'Colin Andrews. Who else?'

'I thought as much. Didn't I tell you to lay off the overseer? Can't you do what you're told and stop trying to make mischief?'

'I'm not trying to make mischief,' she flared. 'That's an absurd thing to say!'

Instead of answering, he suddenly swung his mount about and careered off past the ringing mob of cattle in a cloud of dust.

Keitha watched in amazement, for a moment almost stunned. Away over there she could see Mellie riding —very fast and very cleverly. She was standing in the stirrups, superb control in every line of her strong beautiful body, her hat hanging down her back. Yes, Mellie on a galloping horse was certainly a sight to see! She was chasing a calf, and Keitha watched it run, astonishingly fast for such a stocky little bundle of beef. In fact, she calculated it ran as fast as any bullock. Mellie was trying to bring it round, but the calf was heading for the scrub and refused to turn. Mellie's horse drew closer. In a moment, she would be right on top of it——

Keitha heard Dane shouting something unintelligible, Mellie's concentration relaxed, her horse faltered and in a final dash, the calf reached the safety of the scrub and disappeared.

Now why on earth had Dane done that? Why

hadn't he let Mellie bring that little calf back to the mob?

All the ringers were converging on the camp now. Horses were hobbled and the stockmen, with the peculiar almost pigeontoed gait that came from spending long hours in the saddle, drifted over for their dinner. Col looked around for Keitha and rode towards her. Mellie and Dane were coming in to the camp too, talking to each other furiously and heatedly across the few feet that divided them. Mellie's colour was high and she was scowling, and Dane had lost his customary air of good-humoured confidence.

'What was that all about?' Keitha asked Col.

'What? I didn't see it. Mellie's getting a slating, is she?' No criticism of the boss, nothing but an acutely intelligent look. Col was like Kate Langley in that he appeared to think Dane could do no wrong.

'Why did he interfere with what Mellie was doing?' Keitha wondered—and she wondered it rather loudly. So loudly in fact that it was obvious Dane heard her, for he sent her a sharp frowning look.

A bough shelter had been erected under the trees—possibly for Mellie's comfort—and she and Mellie sat in its shade and enjoyed the same fare as the men. Mellie, her eyes still dark and angry, occasionally raised her voice to join in the general conversation of the men who were some yards away.

'Did Colin ask you to come out? Or did you ask him to bring you?' she asked Keitha after a while. She had not taken a great deal of notice of the English girl, but then she never did.

Keitha, who was feeling stimulated and very much alive, said, 'Colin asked me. Aren't I lucky?'

Mellie stared at her over the large steak she was eating. 'D'you mean coming out to the camp—or coming with him?'

Keitha thought about it. 'A little of each,' she decided. 'I like Col very much.'

Silence. The Mellie burst out, 'Well, I tell you what, I hate Dane Langley—making a fool of me, bawling me out in front of everyone just because I was chasing up a calf!' She looked up as a shadow fell on the ground and Keitha looked up too and saw Dane towering over them. He dropped down on his heels and occupied himself for a minute or two with his steak and damper sandwich, during which time Col Andrews came to make it a foursome. He too settled on his heels, his back against the white bole of the tree. Keitha had noticed that the men out here had a habit of squatting on their heels and somehow always looked very comfortable in that position. These two were no exception. Col's hat was on the back of his head and his blue eyes smiled over at Keitha.

'I'll fetch you two girls a mug of tea in a sec. How's the food?'

'Marvellous,' said Keitha, smiling back at him brightly. There was tension in the air, and she was acutely aware of Dane. For some reason she wanted to impress on him that she was utterly carefree and happy. But Dane was not paying her much attention.

'Having a moan about me, were you, Melanie?' he drawled. 'Think you can chase calves as well as any stockman, do you? Well, let me tell you there's more than one stockman in this outfit has wished he hadn't tried to get the better of a calf. Another few seconds and that little fellow'd have dived under your horse's neck and the three of you would've been tangled up in a nasty heap on the ground.'

'We wouldn't,' retorted Mellie, her face reddening with fresh anger. 'I'd have turned that calf back—or if he wouldn't turn, Skip would have pulled up.'

'You've ridden Skip before, have you?'

'Yes.'

'Chased calves?'

Mellie shrugged. 'I can't remember.'

'You'd remember if you had ... Next time you come to a muster—and that'll be tomorrow—confer long and carefully with your elders and betters upon your choice of a horse. But in any case, the unalterable rule for you is—just don't ever chase a calf.' Mellie glared at him and he added, 'One more thing—don't try to persuade yourself that you know better than I do.'

'Oh, sometimes I hate you, Dane Langley!'

His eyes narrowed. 'That's fine as far as I'm concerned.' A little smile, not altogether pleasant, was on his lips as he got up and strolled nonchalantly towards the camp fire and the tea. Col, looking serious and thoughtful, and not saying a word, followed him.

'Pig,' muttered Mellie—referring apparently to Dane. 'He said I was showing off—that I was a stupid irresponsible exhibitionist.' Her eyes burned.

Keitha, who knew nothing about chasing calves, thought there was a lot to be said for Mellie's fury. Maybe Dane *was* concerned for her well-being; maybe he did know a lot more than an eighteen-year-old girl could know about working cattle. But he didn't know how to handle women. No, thought Keitha to herself, that was one field where the wonderful Dane Langley definitely fell down. He was so arrogant, so sure he knew best, that he didn't stop to think that Mellie was just an excitable sort of overgrown schoolgirl, who still had her pride, and needed treating with tact. Keitha thought he could have handled Mellie very differently and made a lot better job of it.

Then another thought struck her. Was this, after all, some kind of a lovers' tiff? Was Mellie underneath revelling in Dane's brutal, masterful treatment of her, in his careless trampling on her pride? Was the hatred

Mellie expressed just another side of love? She glanced cautiously at the other girl from the shelter of her lashes and saw her sitting there scowling still.

Poor Mellie, she thought suddenly. She looked so young, so bewildered, so unsure of herself.

The men came back with mugs of tea and Mellie took hers ungraciously. Keitha noticed that she drank it down scalding hot as the stockmen did. She herself had to wait for hers to cool.

Mellie refused to look at Dane or to speak to him, and when he strolled off to talk to some of the men, Col said to her quietly, 'Now calm down, Mellie. You know Dane's only concerned about your safety. He doesn't want you killing yourself in his service.'

'His service!' scoffed Mellie. 'Why am I always supposed to do everything he says and never speak up for myself?'

'You're not,' said Col. 'Don't exaggerate.'

'I'm not exaggerating! *You* know I wouldn't have come to harm Col. Why didn't you stick up for me?'

'Dane is the boss,' the overseer said shortly.

'He's not my boss.' Mellie sounded stubborn. 'Not yet—and not ever.'

'Now hold on,' Col interrupted, but Mellie had turned away and Keitha knew she was hiding tears. The big beautiful bouncing Mellie, who had the constitution of an ox, hiding tears! In a moment she got to her feet and wandered off to Skip.

The stockmen were dispersing once more, for this afternoon the beasts to be sold were to be cut out from the mob, and finally taken to the holding yard.

Col asked, 'What would you like to do, Keitha?'

'Don't worry about me. I'll be quite happy sitting here or riding about. I shan't try to round up anything even as small as a calf.'

Col's smile was very restrained. He didn't approve of

even so slight a criticism of the boss.

'A fall over a calf is usually serious—for both horse and rider,' he said. 'Though the calf usually comes out of it all right. By the way, if you decide to go home, be sure to tell someone.'

'I shall,' promised Keitha. She was pretty sure she would not want to go 'home'. She would enjoy herself much more watching the cutting out procedure. She wondered if Dane had come over to select the beasts he wanted for sale, or if he would leave it to Col. She would soon find out.

He left it to Col, and she respected him for that. She spent most of her time watching him from the trees, but he never even glanced her way. Well, he was watching the cutting out pretty closely. Perhaps he had come to check up on the overseer. Or was it to keep that promise he had made to Mellie to see how she was progressing as a stockman? He had done that, all right!

She sat under the bough shelter and watched the stockmen through a haze of red dust that was thickening by the minute. Lazy in the heat, her eyes screwed up against the glare, she was lulled by the shouts of the stockmen and the bellowing of the bullocks, and started when Dane appeared and flung himself down beside her.

'Well, how are things at the outstation?'

'Fine, thank you.' She looked at him and in spite of herself she knew there was reproach in her eyes. He saw it, of course.

'Those great dark eyes of yours have an accusing look,' he said with casual mockery. 'What have I been doing wrong now?'

She chose deliberately to misunderstand. She knew well enough he was thinking of last mail day, but raising her fine eyebrows, she said, 'Surely you must know! You upset Mellie. She was almost in tears.'

'Mellie? Are we to talk about Mellie? Very well then. But I can't take *all* the credit for Mellie's tears. You had a share in provoking them too, I rather think.'

'*I* did?' Keitha was incredulous. 'I certainly did not!'

'You did indeed. But I shouldn't worry too much. All that's wrong with Mellie in the long run is that she's growing up. And about time too. Maybe your coming to Wayaway will serve some purpose after all, as far as Mellie's concerned.'

'I can't think what you're talking about. I hardly see anything of Mellie——'

'Exactly. But you fraternise with Col, don't you? I did tell you to leave him alone. I'll repeat that. You're supposed to be at the outstation to run around for Patty, not to be coming out to the muster with Col Andrews. Is it a usual occurrence?'

'Of course it's not,' said Keitha with annoyance. 'This is the first time. And Mrs Drummond was pleased for me to come. She said it was time I had a day away from work.'

'I don't doubt she was pleased. But couldn't *you* think up some other way of spending your free time?'

She stared at him, feeling the hot colour coming into her face. He could say that to her after so calmly forgetting what he had half promised! She said coldly, 'This way of relaxing appeals to me. Besides, I'm always being warned not to go off alone and get lost, thereby causing a lot of trouble to people who have better things to do——'

He looked amused. 'Come now, it's not only the trouble we're thinking of. You're something very special out here even if you're rather like a hibiscus flower in that we don't expect to enjoy you for long.' There was a pause. Then—'Well, I missed out on checking up on you the other day. Can I put it down in the books, figuratively speaking, that you're relatively happy at the outstation? And if I look you up now and again will you leave Colin alone? I'm afraid I'm not able to provide much personally in the way of excitement for you——'

Keitha looked at him squarely. His attitude hurt. She said deliberately, 'I agree. You're far from able to do that.' It was a rude thing to say and she said it rudely, and felt she had scored a point. It had given her quite a kick to look straight and hard into those mocking blue eyes meanwhile.

She was not surprised that in another minute he left her.

When the cutting out was over, Keitha and Mellie rode at the back of the mob that was being driven to the yards, and now and again Col or Dane, or both, came to join them. Now Dane's very presence did something to Keitha. There was something heady in his nearness so that she was acutely aware of her physical being, of the feel of the reins in her hands, the sun striking on her face, dazzling her eyes. He had nothing at all to say to her, and even that fact seemed to stimulate rather than aggravate her.

Well within Mellie's hearing, she heard him tell Col conversationally, 'If that girl's to be any use on the run then she'll have to be taught to more levelheaded and less of an exhibitionist. What's more, she must obey orders otherwise she'll finish up breaking her pretty little neck and that will be that. If she won't take any notice of you, then leave her at home.'

Col whitened, and Keitha knew he took the implied criticism hard. She was sure he would never allow Mellie to come to any harm.

'I haven't the time to be tutoring you, Mellie,' Dane concluded.

'That suits me,' muttered Mellie rebelliously, though she blinked hard as if tears were close again.

Keitha listened and looked and thought Dane too bossy altogether. She couldn't let it pass and exclaimed in exasperation, 'What on earth is there such a fuss about? What did Mellie do? Why shouldn't she go after a little calf?'

Dane looked at her impatiently. 'Oh, you city girls! Haven't you been paying attention? Do I have to spell it out? I thought you were a reasonably intelligent girl. Don't tell me after what you've heard that *you'd* go chasing after a calf.'

'You let me chase a bullock the other day,' said Keitha. The altercation stimulated her. 'I don't know what grounds you had for thinking I wouldn't come to any harm, seeing I know nothing about working animals.'

'You'd watched. You had a picked horse, and what's more, your pride wouldn't have let you fall,' said Dane, and capped that off with a final, 'And I was there.'

'Wonderful you,' muttered Mellie, and suddenly dug her heels into her horse's side and raced up at the side of the mob.

Dane gave Col no more than a look and the overseer followed her.

'Wonderful you,' thought Keitha, and looked at Dane maliciously.

'Why don't you keep out of our domestic squabbles?' he asked curtly. 'Stick to what concerns you— your continental cookery and your long letters to England. You're certainly having some fun, but just don't start making too big a nuisance of yourself before you go running back home.'

Keitha felt furious. She had been rude, but he was ruder. Yet he was supposed to be such a polite and considerate host. Well, he was host no more, it was true. She didn't know what he was. Reluctant employer, perhaps! Her cheeks were flushed, and she knew she must look a sight, her face stained with dust and perspiration. But at least her shirt, unlike Mellie's, was well and truly tucked in! She didn't know why Dane was being so hard to get on with. For good measure, he added just then, 'Don't forget to let me know, will you, just as soon as you've had your fill of this part of sunny Queensland, and I'll put you on the plane personally.'

'Will you!' thought Keitha angrily. Mellie's words came into her mind and she echoed them to herself with feeling. 'Sometimes I hate you, Dane Langley.' That 'sometimes' was the trouble. What had got into him this evening? She told herself it would be a long time before she gave him the opportunity of seeing her off from the Gulf Country. When she did go, she would go without his even knowing it—if she could find a way...

CHAPTER EIGHT

OVER two weeks went by and she saw nothing at all of Dane, though she knew Mellie had been over to the home station once or twice. It was obvious now that he was deliberately avoiding her and she felt unutterably frustrated and restless.

She wrote a letter to Donn that had been in her mind for some time. She knew now that she had never really loved him, otherwise she could not have willingly gone so far away from him as she had chosen to do. When you really loved, you wanted to be near the one you loved, no matter that the circumstances. She was sure of that.

She wrote, 'You say you love me, Donn. You say it over and over, so easily, so lightly. Yet you can't bring yourself to say "Marry me". I've put my own interpretation on that. You said once that living together would be the same as being married—that for you and me it would be for ever. It's not very flattering really, you know. Because I believe in marriage. In fact, I believe in a lot of the things that you've discarded. I just don't belong in your world, so I think we'd better say goodbye to each other. I loved knowing you, Donn, but I've somehow changed since I've been out here. I could never go back—in any sense of the word... Don't hold that job for me. I know you'll find someone else to love and I hope it will be someone whose ideas are not as old-fashioned as mine...'

Her letter would have to wait for next mail day to go, but she wouldn't change her mind about sending it. She didn't think she would ever go back to London, and if she did, it would certainly not be to Donn. She was under some sort of a spell out here. There was something mesmeric in the long sunny days. The heat from the sky and the shimmer of the sun-drenched plains danced like a haunting melody through her mind—a melody that burst into a crescendo of sound and colour at sundown, when the birds filled the sky as they came down to the lagoon for water.

'If you demand compensation for living in the out-back'—Dane's words came back into her mind every evening—'then sundown's one of them.'

Perhaps her life would come back into some sort of perspective when she returned to the coast, but just now she couldn't even contemplate a time when she would fly east.

Sometimes as she lay sleepless in her bedroom, listening to the thud of mangoes on the roof, and the screeching of the fruit bats breaking the deep throbbing silence of the outback night, she wondered what she wanted from life. If perhaps in her heart she knew the answer to that question she refused to acknowledge it.

Col taught her to ride the motorbike one Sunday, and she found it not difficult to master. Patty approved of the lessons, though Keitha knew Dane would not have done so, suspicious that she was trying to enmesh the overseer in some fleeting affair that would disturb the peace of the cattle station—if peace existed! Keitha saw undercurrents of unrest everywhere—in Patty, in Mellie, in Col and certainly in herself.

Col didn't take her out on the run again, though Patty vaguely suggested more than once that he might do so. Keitha wondered if he were acting on the boss's orders, and thought it extremely likely.

One night after dinner, she took a stroll in the garden, and as she came back through the soft warm darkness that lay like silk against her bare arms and legs she could hear Mellie playing the piano. She had been over to the Wayaway homestead that day, and it was a Beethoven sonata she was playing. Keitha paused to listen. Mellie didn't play well—there was not a single piece that she had perfected. And this sonata—she was having a terrible struggle with it! Was it for Dane—whom she had said she hated—that she was trying to master it? That seemed utterly ludicrous and unrealistic. By no stretch of the imagination could one imagine Dane choosing to listen to Mellie's efforts when he had some beautiful recordings. Unless, of course, Dane were madly in love with Mellie. But he was not madly in love with Mellie. On the other hand, he was possibly calmly and coolly waiting to see how she 'shaped up'.

A voice broke into her reflections.

'A penny for your thoughts.' It was Col, lounging in a garden chair near the papaw trees.

'Oh, you startled me. I was just listening to Mellie.' She took a chair near him. 'She'd never take a prize, would she?'

'Maybe not. But I like to listen to her. There's something very nostalgic in the sound of a piano being played in a house at night. Imperfection has more appeal for me than technical brilliance—there's something of Mellie's heart coming over from that music.'

Quite obviously Col thought more of the person who was playing than he did of the music! The things Mellie was doing to that sonata were pretty well unforgivable, if you liked Beethoven. Col was protected because he was thinking of Mellie and her heart.

'I wonder how she got on with Dane over at the home station today,' she mused aloud. 'Does she still hate him?' She hardly knew why she asked it except that it gave her pleasure to talk about Dane even in-directly.

Col laughed. 'Never in a million years. Mellie says things like that—she doesn't mean them. Dane hurt her pride a bit, that was all. But the reprimand was necessary,' he added quickly. 'She takes a lot of chances she shouldn't.'

'Why don't *you* stop her?'

There was a slight pause. Then—'I watch her,' said Col quietly. 'I wouldn't let anything happen to Mellie ... By the way, did you know there's to be a picnic at the Tyrone Park border muster tomorrow?'

'No.' Keitha's heart began to beat fast. 'Who's going?'

'About everyone, I guess. Dane and Kate—Bill—the O'Boyles—us——'

'Me?' interrupted Keitha quickly.

'Well, of course.'

Keitha was suddenly filled with a wild excitement. She would see Dane again! The thought was there in her mind before she could censure it. All right, so she wanted to see Dane. That didn't mean she was falling in love with him. He was just part of the general spell of the outback—he dominated life out here whether he was present or not. She asked Col eagerly, 'What *is* a border muster, Col? Tell me about it so I won't look a fool.'

'You're no fool, Keitha,' Col assured her. 'You could work it out for yourself if you did a bit of thinking.' But he explained obligingly, 'As you know, fences are practically non-existent hereabouts, which means that cattle from one station are bound to stray on to the neighbouring runs. It's only in comparatively small numbers, though, because except during the Wet they stick within a comfortable distance of the waterhole they habitually use. Tyrone Park is mustering at the

Blue Waterhole near Wayaway's boundary—up this end of the run, that is—so they've let us know and Dane will send along a few stockmen. Any cattle with the Wayaway brand, and any calves with cows that carry our brand, will be cut out of the mob they muster and we'll bring them home and brand them next day. Do get it?'

'Yes,' Keitha was listening intently. 'Go on.'

'Well, that's about it. Cleanskins—that is, un-branded cattle—stay on Tyrone Park and will be marked with their brand. If the muster were on our side of the border, it would be the other way around, of course. The cleanskins would stay with us and henceforth belong with our herds.'

'I see. Yes, I expect I could have worked that out . . . Whose idea was the picnic, Col?'

'Justine O'Boyle's. Should be a good day. You'll enjoy it, Keitha—it'll be something else to add to your little store of Queensland experiences.' And though Col didn't mean it that way, his words had the effect of instantly, and rather dampeningly, making Keitha realise anew that they all considered her an outsider.

And she wanted rather badly to belong.

It was Keitha who prepared the picnic basket the following morning. Patty Drummond came out to the kitchen just as she finished packing away the last piece of fruit.

'I'll take that out to the car, Keitha, if you want to go upstairs and fetch your things, and then we must be on our way. We're already later than I promised Dane we'd be,' she added, glancing at her watch.

Keitha hoped that she wasn't going to be blamed for not having the picnic basket packed earlier and quickly took off the apron she had tied on over her clean jeans. Col had left the homestead early as usual and was going to meet them at the Blue Waterhole.

Keitha was all but out the kitchen door when a dis-
traught lubra appeared, a yelling child of about
twelve months clutched in her arms. She was a shy girl
called Oobi, with whom Keitha had made friends at
the aboriginal quarters, and blood from her baby's leg
had stained her skirt and was still flowing.

Keitha reached for the child and asked quickly,
'What happened, Oobi? Let's have a look at that
leg...' In a moment she was able to say reassuringly,
'It's not such a deep cut. But there's some glass in it.
We'll have to get that out.' She turned enquiringly to
Patty, to make sure she wanted to leave it to Keitha,
and to her surprise found the other woman sitting in a
chair, her face, deathly white, lowered into her hands.

'It's not serious, Mrs Drummond.'

'I know—I know. But I could never stand the sight
of blood. I'll be all right in a minute.'

Keitha thought it an unfortunate weakness in one
whose proud boast was that she was born and bred a
countrywoman. By the time she had fetched a bowl
and the first aid kit from the locked cupboard upstairs,
Patty was more or less in control of herself again.
Johnnie was still howling, and Oobi was weeping in
sympathy.

'I want to leave in five minutes, Keitha,' Patty said.
'So be quick, won't you? Pick the glass out and let
Oobi do the dressing herself. The aboriginals have
been told about antiseptics and so on often enough.'

'I'll be as quick as I can, Mrs Drummond,' said
Keitha. It was going to take her a lot longer than five
minutes to deal with this cut. What was more, she was
going to find out how dirty the glass had been and she
was going to clean and dress it herself.

Mrs Drummond left the kitchen, taking the picnic
basket with her, and Keitha worked quickly and
gently on the baby's leg, removing glass and trying to

soothe the young mother at the same time. She talked cheerfully until her weeping had stopped. Johnnie had quietened too and removed his fat brown fists from huge dark eyes to peep at what was happening to his knee.

'Now tell me how it happened, Oobi, and where the glass came from.'

'Him clean fella bottle, missus—get broken up longa the floor and Johnnie he crawl that way.'

'We'll go and have a look presently.'

In another minute Mellie came into the kitchen. 'We can't wait all day, Keitha. If you want to come to the picnic you'd better come now. Oobi will be all right. It's only a little cut, isn't it? Mother says you'll have the girls spoiled if you do everything for them.'

Keitha looked up.

'There's still a bit of glass here. I'll have to get it out—it's a bit tricky. Can't you hang on for a bit?'

Mellie looked helpless. 'Mother says not. She told Dane what time we'd be there and we're late already. He likes people to stick to what they say.'

'Regardless? Well then, you'd better go without me,' said Keitha. Of course she didn't want to miss the picnic, but Johnnie was twelve months old and he was an important little fellow. He took priority over any picnic. She looked up at Mellie, who stood biting her lip nervously. Poor Mellie! She was still little more than a schoolgirl in many ways, and Keitha thought with a trace of pity, 'You'll never grow up till you get away from that quietly domineering mother of yours.'

She said brightly, 'Cheer up, Mellie. If I feel like it I'll come over to the picnic on one of the motorbikes. Someone will tell me the way. I can't leave this job half done.'

'I'll tell Mother,' said Mellie. 'I'll persuade her to wait.'

But her persuasive powers were not great enough, for only five minutes later Keitha heard the station wagon leave the yard. She really had hoped they would wait for her, and her heart sank. But she pushed her disappointment aside and gave her mind entirely to the task in hand.

Now that there was no hurry, she took her time, and finally it was half an hour before she was ready to go. At the aboriginal quarters, the other women had come clustering around shyly, giggling and talking. Keitha checked up on Oobi's story of clean glass, and then told them that she wanted to go to the Blue Waterhole on Tyrone Park. They all knew where it was, but none of them could tell her how to get there. Dolly, one of the housegirls, said, 'You ask Tucker, missus. That old fella he knows everything. He tell you real good how to get there.'

Tucker was in the vegetable garden. He thought long and deeply and then he took Keitha out to the yard in front of the homestead garden, and with much pointing and with references to such landmarks as 'yella stump like big fella dingo', 'trees like old men talkum', and 'plenty big anthills walkum through scrub', described how to reach the Blue Waterhole.

Keitha listened attentively, and having thanked him fetched the motorbike from the garage. Her need to get to the picnic—to see Dane Langley again—was so urgent that she persuaded herself she would find the way from Tucker's somewhat picturesque directions.

The first part of the track was not hard to follow, for the station car had been over it a short time ago and the long grasses were flattened. But where there was no spear grass there was no track, for the ground was as hard as iron. Then she spied that stump like a big yellow dingo and headed towards it elatedly. Beyond that was a sandy stretch and she once again picked up

137

the station wagon's tracks.

She was doing fine! It was certainly an uncomfortably hot and bumpy ride and she was a tiny bit afraid of the motorbike, but she would get there, on that she was absolutely determined.

At last away across the plain she could see a group of trees hunched and bent—'like old men talkum'. That exactly described them. Tucker certainly had an apt and memorable way of describing landmarks that made them unmistakable.

By the time she had reached the distant trees, she was dusty and parched and quite sure that she must look a sight. A few cattle that had been standing in the shade began to disperse at her approach to more trees that grew around a small waterhole, and she pulled up at a safe distance and watched them. The sight of the water with its muddy banks and reflections of tree and sky made her long for a drink. She knew that she should have brought a flask of water with her, but in her eagerness to be on her way she had not given it a thought.

Well, she had better look for those anthills. But first she decided to tidy herself a little, and using the mirror from the small holdall she had brought with her, she wiped some of the dust from her face with a tissue, combed her hair and applied a little fresh lipstick. Then from the shelter of the 'old men' trees she began to scan the plain for anthills walking through the scrub. There was scrub all right—a great wide belt of it at the far end of a long stretch of open plain—but she had no idea whether the anthills were left, right or centre.

The best thing to do seemed to be to study the ground for wheel marks, and this she began to do. She hunted for what seemed a very long time and was beginning to despair when something made her look up.

Out towards the far end of that belt of scrub was a cloud of red dust and it was whirling along in her direction. It was surely not a willywilly, and it was moving too fast to be cattle. Soon she heard the hum of a motor and the dust revealed itself as a Land-Rover.

Keitha felt as excited as a shipwrecked sailor who has sighted a sail. Her first thought was that she would get a drink—she was as parched as that—her second was to wonder who it could be. Whoever it was, they would be able to put her on the right track for Tyrone Park and the Blue Waterhole, that was for sure.

Another three minutes and her heart began to pound. She knew who it was. It was Dane Langley.

He pulled up two yards from where she stood, got out of the Rover and came to stand and stare at her, hands on his hips, broad-brimmed hat slanted rakishly over his eyes.

'So it's the bush orchid rearing its pretty head.'

She flushed. 'What brings you here, Dane Langley?'

'Why, you do, Keitha Godwin. What else? I missed you at the muster and Patty said you wouldn't be along. I was going to the outstation to fetch you—it wouldn't do for you to miss the picnic.' His mouth quirked. 'However, I'd forgotten about your determined spirit. Of course you had to try to make it on your own, and here you are—lost.'

'I'm not lost at all,' said Keitha. 'So you needn't have bothered about me.'

His blue eyes looked her over quizzically. 'I can't seem to help bothering about you, honey. And if you're not lost, it's amazing. You really should have come with the others, you know. Why didn't you?'

'One of the babies had had an accident——'

Understanding showed on his face. 'And accidents make Patty squeamish, I know. But they'd have waited for you, surely.'

'I told them not to,' she said quickly. 'I told Mellie I'd get there if I wanted to.'

'And you did want to?'

A slow flush suffused her cheeks. 'Yes, of course ... If you have any water, I'd like a drink. I forgot to bring a flask.'

'You *were* in a hurry!' He offered no further criticism, but fetched his waterbag and poured her a mug of cool water. She drank it down thirstily so that her eyes watered, and thought it was the most delicious drink she had ever tasted.

'Shall we be on our way now?' he asked conversationally when she had finished.

'Yes.'

He waited, but she did not move. In her heart, she had been very relieved to see him come. She didn't really know the way. Even if she found those anthills, she didn't know what came after that. She could follow him now, at all events, and he need never know.

'After you, Miss Godwin,' he said softly, his eyes mocking.

After her! She felt furiously angry with him. Was he determined on proving her a liar if he could? Couldn't he—just this once—be a gentleman and go ahead?

As if he had read her thoughts he said, with a tilt of his brows, 'Or would you rather follow in my dust?'

She bit her lip. She had misjudged him.

Suddenly he relented.

'Look, honey, we'll leave the motorbike here. Somebody can pick it up on the way home. You hop in the car with me. That way, you won't arrive at the picnic shaken to pieces.' Now the screwed-up electric blue eyes had softened, and like Mellie she found herself turning away to hide sudden tears. Because after all, she was hot and tired and just a little bit frightened and now it was going to be all right.

He didn't speak again until they were travelling across the plain towards the scrub. Then he said musingly, 'Come to think of it, you've quite a bit of initiative and courage for a city girl. One can't help admiring you for it.'

'Thank you, Mr Langley.' Her voice was husky though she had herself under control again. 'It's nice of you to praise me. Because sometimes I get the distinct feeling that you'd as soon I left Wayaway.'

'Hmm. Dice the formality bit anyhow, honey. Trouble is, I get the feeling that you're definitely *going* to quit Wayaway.'

How did she take that? Did he mean she was going to leave of her own volition? Or did he mean that he would see to it that she did leave? She was floundering and uncertain and just now felt completely at his mercy. Suddenly she longed to lean against him and to say, 'I surrender. I don't want to fight you any longer, I just want to rest here—near you—and not think at all.'

That proved of course that she was crazy. Maybe it was what happened to all the girls. They just gave up trying to work out where they stood with him—as long as they could be there it was enough. Except for Mellie, who had said, 'I hate you.' Mellie had spirit. Did he like spirit? Well, even if he did, he couldn't care less about Keitha Godwin. She was someone passing through. When she had gone he would forget her. And just how soon would that be?

Soon they had reached the Blue Waterhole and she hadn't even looked out for those anthills. There was a great mob of lowing cattle and dust everywhere. There were stockmen from Tyrone Park and a few from Wayaway, shouts of laughter, the cracking of stockwhips. Away under some trees was the picnic camp, and Kate was sitting there placidly drawing, an outsize sketch pad on her knees. Keitha smiled at the sight of Kate. There was someone who would be glad to see her!

Patty Drummond was there too and another woman —Mrs O'Boyle, probably.

As Dane drove slowly past the mob, giving it a wide berth, a girl came riding out of the dust. She pulled on her horse's reins and laughed as she cantered up and bent down towards the Rover. It was Dusty—Justine, rather—the girl Keitha had seen at the airstrip, and she looked just as attractive now as she had then. There was scarcely a dust-streak on her face and her sleek, silver-brown hair was flipped neatly back from under a black ranch-type hat that had a silver chin strap. Her eyes were a clean grey-green, and she wore a pink shirt and smart black jeans.

'Hi, Dane! So you got the reluctant girl.' She walked her horse alongside the car until it came to a halt, then swung herself lightly down from the saddle, tossed her reins over a bough, and almost the moment Dane put his feet to the ground her hand was through his arm.

'So you're the girl who's got us all curious,' she exclaimed as Keitha stepped from the car. Her eyes flicked over Keitha quickly and efficiently, and Keitha was glad she had made time for that little bit of sprucing up out on the plain. 'I was beginning to wonder if any of us would meet you at all before you left the place. And you know, you really mustn't go home without saying hello to us all over the radio schedule. Must she, Dane?'

'That's up to Keitha,' said Dane. 'This is Justine O'Boyle, honey, as no doubt you already know. You'll have gathered Justine knows all about you—probably more than you know yourself, if I know anything about the galah sessions.'

The three of them strolled together towards the picnic camp, and Keitha wondered why Justine took it so much for granted that she would be leaving Wayaway cattle run soon. They were well out of range of the stirring dust now, and Keitha greeted Kate and was introduced to Mrs O'Boyle. She received a not over-enthusiastic welcome from Patty Drummond, who nevertheless lost no time in suggesting that now she was here, she might help to serve out the picnic lunch.

'I'll leave you to it, girls,' said Dane. 'See you at lunch.'

Mellie had ridden up. She was leading Dane's horse and Keitha spent a moment watching the two of them ride off together. She wondered if Mellie had quite forgotten her avowal of hatred and if she was after all in love with the boss of Wayaway. Beyond the dust that hovered over the mob of cattle, she thought she could see Col—and Bill. Justine had decided not to rejoin the muster but to stay and help with the lunch.

A trestle table, brought from Tyrone Park, had been put up and spread with a red and white check cloth. The picnic baskets were opened and Keitha discovered they were to picnic in style—there were china plates and cups, and silver knives and forks. No beef and damper today, though the stockmen would have their usual hearty fare, for at the other end of the waterhole Keitha could see that the camp cook had lit a fire.

Justine said casually, 'You must have made quite a hit with Dane to have him go to the outstation to pick you up. Patty Drummond was livid!'

'Was she? I don't think she need have been.'

'One wouldn't think so, seeing that you'll be gone before we know where we are,' agreed Justine, who was making no more than a show of helping with the picnic. 'Were you really not going to bother coming? Or did you hope that Dane would go and fetch you?'

Keitha, who hadn't cared much for that suggestion that she would so soon be gone, flushed with annoyance. 'If you really must know, I was well on the way here on a motorbike.'

Justine looked at her disbelievingly. 'A London girl looking for the Blue Waterhole on a motorbike! You'd have been lost for sure ... Well, wasn't it nice for you that Dane came to the rescue? He's quite a pearl, isn't he?'

Keitha thought it a strange way to describe the attractions of the boss of Wayaway, but lightly agreed that Dane was a pearl. Which didn't seem to please Justine as much as it should have.

'I suppose you have at least a passing interest in him.'

Keitha smiled brightly across the table that was beginning to look very attractive with its bowls of salads and platters of cold meats. 'I understand he more or less belongs to Mellie.'

Justine fished a stack of good-looking glasses from a deep basket and began to set them out on the table. 'Oh, that's a load of rubbish. It's only what Patty would like. Dane couldn't possibly marry Mellie, she's far too simple and countrified for a man of his discrimination. Of course Mellie *tries*—she's trying now —because Patty's brought her up to think it's expected of her. Patty's father was head stockman on Wayaway once upon a time. Did you know that? Poor Patty has some sort of inferiority complex. She's quite sure that if Mellie married Dane it would prove that she was better than anyone in the whole of the Gulf Country. And wouldn't *that* be lovely?'

Their conversation ended there, for all the musterers were now converging on the camp or on the picnic site. To Keitha's surprise, Bill Sutton made straight for her and greeted her as keenly as if they had

144

a date. 'So you made it, Keitha! That's terrific. Anything I can do?'

'Not a thing, thanks, Bill. We have everything under control.'

He moved away momentarily and soon the picnic was in full swing. Justine stuck determinedly to Dane, openly wooing him, and Bill Sutton stuck just about as closely to Keitha, having somewhat strangely deputised himself to make a fuss of her. He assured her that if she wanted to do some riding during the afternoon he would see she got a safe horse.

'You can come with me if you want to ride around and kid yourself you're taking part in the muster.'

'Thank you very much,' she said ironically. But she reflected that quite possibly she would take up his offer, for it looked as though Dane was going to be fully occupied with Justine. Mellie too was hovering indecisively and worriedly on the sidelines.

'I'm a little surprised you came to the picnic, Bill,' Keitha said a little later.

He shrugged. 'Maybe *you* came to the picnic. *I* came to the muster. But don't forget what you promised me, will you, about coming over to Wayaway later on. I notice Justine's brought all her gear. She'll be riding back with our outfit after the day's work is finished.'

'I'll see what I can do since I promised,' agreed Keitha. 'But it may not work out.'

When lunch was over, Keitha set to work clearing away the debris and repacking the crockery and cutlery. Kate returned to her drawing, Patty considered it her right to relax and Mrs O'Boyle looked so hot and tired that Keitha could not imagine letting her do anything but sit down and rest.

'Don't you want to join the others?' she asked Justine who had stayed to help her.

'Oh, I'll get hold of Dane in a minute or two.

There's no sense in overdoing it, and I like to stay cool and calm and feminine at least some of the time. Look at poor old Mellie! She's having marvellous fun, but doesn't she look a mess? How on earth can she hope to fascinate Dane that way? It's a wonder Patty doesn't stop her.'

Keitha watched Mellie racing past hot on the trail of a wayward bullock. Not far behind was Col and his eyes were on Mellie rather than on the bullock. Mellie did look a mess, but she was happy and obviously didn't give a thought to her appearance. And, Keitha reflected, to Col's eyes at least she probably looked radiantly beautiful.

'Someone will come back for us now we've cleared all this up,' said Justine. 'Or would you rather sit around in the shade with the oldies and save your lovely complexion?'

'If you can take it, so can I,' said Keitha cheerfully.

'Who do you expect to come back for *you*?' Justine wanted to know. She was arranging her pretty hair under the smart black hat and her grey-green eyes were not entirely friendly.

'Bill said I could stick with him.'

'Really? You're doing very nicely with Bill, aren't you? I'm beginning to suspect you're quite a collector of scalps.'

'Are you? Then you're wrong.'

'Oh, I don't know. First Dane Langley, then Bill Sutton. And then of course there's always what's-his-name——' She paused and leaned down to remove a spike of spear grass from her boot. And as at that moment Dane arrived leading two horses, Keitha didn't have the opportunity to ask who what's-his-name might be. Just as well perhaps, as there was something rather disagreeable about the trend the conversation was taking.

'Do you girls want to ride?'

'Keitha's waiting for Bill,' said Justine instantly. 'But I'm coming with you, Dane.'

He tilted a quizzical look down at Keitha. 'I just can't keep up with you, Miss Godwin——'

'Don't try,' she said coolly, but as she watched him ride off with Justine, her heart contracted and she was aware of a spasm of acute jealousy.

Nevertheless, she enjoyed the afternoon once Bill came to collect her. She loved the horses and the riding and the sight of the cattle. She even loved the dust. And the excitement of riding around the outskirts of the mob and watching Michael O'Boyle's skill as he cut out the animals he wanted: the cleanskins that were to stay on Tyrone Park, the bullocks and cows— some of them with unbranded calves—that belonged on the Wayaway run and would be taken back there later on. She was glad she had got Col to explain to her what it was all about, so that she was able to watch intelligently. She loved the heat pouring down from the sky and the shining waters of the Blue Waterhole where reflections of grey green trees and blue sky alternated with patches of beautiful lotus lilies ... She loved smoko when the billy was boiled and the men filled their quartpots and the picnickers drank mugs of steaming hot tea and ate the cakes and scones and biscuits brought from the homesteads.

She had no further talk with Dane, though she watched him whenever she could. Bill stuck to her pretty closely and Justine stuck to Dane and Mellie seemed pretty well unaware of anyone. It occurred to Keitha that she was possibly more in love with the run than with anyone on it, and in that perhaps she was like Dane...

It was nearly sundown when the work was finished and the stockmen from Wayaway began to drive their mob slowly towards the nearest waterhole on the station run. Dane and Bill, Mellie and Col stayed with the mob, and Justine got into the Land-Rover with Kate.

They all met up later at the outstation where Bill and Dane left their horses. They came inside briefly for a drink and Dane said, 'Seeing we're to have a house-guest for a few days, I think we'll have to arrange a party. What do you say, Kate? You must all come over and stay a night or two with us.'

Keitha thought she must be imagining it, but it seemed to her that Dane looked especially long at her across the lamplit room. Then the book-keeper said unexpectedly, 'Terrific! What sort of a dancer are you, Keitha?'

She felt herself colouring and barely heard Kate remark to Patty, 'We'll arrange it between us over the transceiver. But we'll make it soon.'

'Before Keitha goes,' said Justine with a tinge of malice, and Patty added sweetly, 'I expect Justine will only stay a day or two.'

'You hope,' thought Keitha aware of the meaning behind the sweetness. Yet she, crazily, hoped so too.

CHAPTER NINE

FROM that night, Keitha could think of nothing but the coming visit to Wayaway. Dane was there in her mind whether she liked it or not, and she couldn't seem to get him out of it. Nor could she stop herself from thinking about Justine O'Boyle—riding with the boss, dining with him at night, listening with him to music on the dark verandah. Maybe walking down by the lagoon with him at sundown. What would she accomplish? She was a very attractive girl, and the first time Keitha had seen her, that day at the Tyrone Park airstrip, she had more or less openly avowed her intention of breaking through his defences. Having seen her in action at the picnic, Keitha suspected that she would stop at nothing. And at present she had the field to herself.

Still, the airpilot had been right when he said Dane Langley was a hard nut to crack. Besides which he was no fool. No girl was going to win him by tricks or flattery. Whether Mellie Drummond would win him because she had 'shaped up' well was quite another matter. Or did he have a vulnerable heart after all beneath that arrogant, self-confident exterior?

Keitha simply didn't know, and was more and more inclined to wish she had left Wayaway long ago. In which case, would it still be Donn she dreamed about at night? She didn't think so. No—somehow in any case she was sure that the end result of her coming to Queensland would have been to get Donn out of her system. Perhaps it had been her subconscious reason for leaving England in the first place. Because what Donn had offered her was not good enough. It had been altogether a shoddy deal to hand out to the girl he professed to love. She was glad she had sent him that letter—that it was all over. And while he might be hurt at first, she was pretty certain he would get over it quickly.

She didn't know quite what she expected of the visit to Wayaway, yet as soon as the date was set, she began feverishly planning what clothes she would take; dreamed of dancing with Dane, of going riding with him the way she had in her first week on the run. All as if neither Mellie nor Justine existed. She hoped that Bill Sutton would not try to monopolise her. Why did he want her to come to the home station while Justine was there? She was very much inclined to believe that it was Justine who was the cause of his embittered outlook on life and on women in particular.

When at last the day came for them to leave the outstation, her nerves were taut. They set out in the station wagon in the late afternoon, with Col driving. He would stay away only one night, returning to the outstation the next day. Patty, who did not want Keitha along but couldn't do a thing about it, had given her a little talk during the afternoon—a talk that made the girl feel rather like Cinderella!

'Now you do understand, Keitha, that though you have been invited as a guest to come with us, you will still be working for me, and you shan't be able to go gallivanting about just as you please. Three of us will give Kate extra work and you will have to do your share of it.'

'Yes, of course, Mrs Drummond,' agreed Keitha readily. She would in any case have offered to help Kate. It constantly surprised her that Mrs Drummond didn't sack her, for though she worked hard enough at the homestead, she was aware that her presence was not necessary as far as the older woman was concerned.

Perhaps while they were under Dane's roof she would manage to convince him that Keitha's services were no longer required. And then what? Would Dane be more inclined to agree about that now?

Keitha had an intuitive feeling that matters were coming to a head at last, but just now she could not bear to contemplate the thought of leaving Wayaway —of never seeing Dane Langley again. In fact, she refused to look further ahead than the next day...

Darkness fell as they drove across the plains. The sky was as clear and starry as ever, but away out on the rim of the horizon lightning danced, and now and again a long low growl of thunder could be heard.

'Not long now till the Wet,' said Col. Keitha sat in the front beside him. In the back of the station wagon, behind the other passengers, was such a mountain of luggage that one had the impression Patty Drummond meant to stay with the Langleys almost indefinitely. 'We'll have to get our mob on the road soon for the sales, and send out the trucks for next year's supplies. Before we know it the rivers will be flooding.'

The Wet, Keitha knew, lasted for about three months of the year, and during that time about forty inches of rain would fall in torrents, filling the rivers and creeks and making the land break out in a cover of unbelievable green.

'What a pity you will never see the green grasses on our pastures, Keitha,' Patty remarked from the back seat. She didn't sound as though she thought it was a pity at all. 'You'll be back in England long before that, though.'

Keitha's heart sank. Her conjectures had been right. Patty was going to put her case to Dane, and she would have to go. But it would not be back to England.

She said restrainedly, 'It would be wonderful to see

the Gulf Country after the Wet. And who knows—maybe I shall.'

Patty Drummond sniffed. 'I very much doubt it. Very much ...'

When they reached the homestead, it was Justine who came forward across the verandah at Dane's side to greet the guests—like a hostess—while Kate stood to one side, though her smile for Keitha was full of welcome and friendliness.

The mere sight of Dane—the brief touch of his fingers on her hand, the oddly wary smile in his eyes—made Keitha's nerves jangle.

She was given her old room, and there, after a quick refreshing shower, she changed with hands that trembled into one of her London dresses—a bright orange affair—and made up her face with rather more care than usual, adding eye-shadow and mascara. She had not missed the fact that Justine was looking particularly glamorous in a long-skirted gown of a clinging, filmy material in one of the newest designs. Mellie too would be at her best in one of the new dresses Patty had made so professionally for her.

When Keitha went into the dining room, she found the dinner table formally set with a starched white cloth and candles in silver candlesticks. There were crystal goblets and wine was to be served with the meal. Some of this was Justine's doing, she was sure—though not, as it happened, the cooking.

When they were seated she was sure, too, that Justine had planned the seating arrangements. Dane sat at one end of the long table, Kate at the other. On one side were Patty, Col and Mellie, with Patty next to Dane. Opposite them were Justine, Bill and Keitha, Justine, of course, being beside Dane. This arrangement made Keitha do a little thinking. Justine had put herself between Dane and Bill. And she had put Mellie next to Col. Keitha suspected that Justine didn't very much like the attention Bill had paid her at the border muster—she had even made a crack about collecting scalps. But she was more interested in underlining an association between Mellie and Col than she was in keeping Keitha away from Bill. Keitha didn't really count for much in the order of things as far as Justine was concerned, because she would soon be gone. Keitha had no idea what made Justine so sure of this, but sure of it she was judging from various remarks she had made the other day.

After the wine was poured and dinner had begun, Dane commented with a touch of irony, 'We certainly are festive tonight! Do I detect your hand here, Justine? Or is it Kate who has suddenly become romantic?'

Justine smile at him in the candlelight, which put lovely lights in her eyes and hair—and in Mellie's too, Keitha noticed.

'A little bit of gracious living, Dane—so we can make believe we're in Brisbane or Sydney instead of in the outback.'

'The outback will do me every time, Justine,' said Dane. He indicated the dinner plates. 'The fare's outback at all events. But definitely! There's no mistaking good Wayaway beef, and Mrs Dimmick knows how to cook it. Eh, Col? Or have you developed a taste for fancy cooking lately?'

Col grinned. 'I just like good food well cooked, Dane. And we're lucky our womenfolk know how to deal with it.'

Justine looked slightly displeased that the talk had switched from atmosphere—created by her—to food, cooked to perfection by somebody else. She said maliciously, '*Our* womenfolk, Col? That phrase has a proprietorial ring about it.' She smiled innocently at

Mellie. 'I didn't know you found time to cook the meals at the outstation, Mellie.'

Mellie went scarlet and Patty looked infuriated by Justine's insinuation. Mellie Drummond was earmarked for Dane, not for Col! But before she could speak, Kate put in smoothly, 'Keitha does the cooking at the outstation these days, Justine. And Dane tells me she does it very well indeed.'

'But not for much longer,' said Patty, smiling sweetly now, while it was Justine who looked put out. Keitha would have liked to ask Patty exactly what she meant, but it was hardly the time to do so at a dinner party. Dane at all events created a diversion by getting up to refill the wine glasses. And Bill, who was the only one who had offered nothing so far in the way of conversation, asked, 'Is it true? Are you really leaving us soon, Keitha?'

Keitha looked at Patty. 'I don't know,' she said cautiously. Dane was filling her glass and he said, in her ear, so softly that only Kate could have heard it apart from Keitha, '*Don't* you know, Keitha Godwin? We shall have to talk about that.'

Keitha's heart thudded. Such a talk could lead in only one direction. She was going to be finally and permanently excluded from Wayaway. As far as she was concerned, the rest of the dinner was spoilt.

Later, they went on to the verandah to dance. Justine had unearthed a few dance records, and having put one on the record player made no bones about asking Dane if they would start the ball rolling. Bill claimed Keitha, and Col, satisfied that the boss had had first choice, danced with Mellie.

In no time at all, Justine and Dane disappeared into the garden. If Patty Drummond appeared agitated about this, it was nothing to the way Keitha was feeling and she was furious with herself. When would she ever learn sense? She forced her attention back to Bill, who had been making no effort at conversation, and remarked lightly, 'You're a good dancer, Bill. You must have done a fair bit of it in your time. What happened to make you go sour on the fair sex?' She would never have asked such a personal question if she hadn't been talking for the sole purpose of keeping her mind occupied, and was quite astounded at his instant and savage reply.

'Haven't you guessed yet? You must be as blind as the boss ... Justine O'Boyle happened to me.'

She looked up at him thoughtfully. 'I thought it might be that—I didn't think you were paying me so much attention for my own sake. But what went wrong, Bill? Is it the pecking order I hear about that holds you back?'

'I don't give a damn for the pecking order,' he said, his eyes hard. 'Miss Justine O'Boyle simply hasn't looked my way since I came here. And I'm not going to crawl for any woman. When I fell for her in Brisbane, I was fool enough to think it was the great outback that was calling her when she wouldn't commit herself and insisted on coming home to Tyrone Park. To please her, I got myself a job out here, and what did I find?' He stopped dancing and looked down at Keitha. 'She's just one more of several stupid females busting themselves to get the boss to fall in love with them. Can you wonder that my opinion of women has reached an all-time low? I'm quitting this outfit. I'll be back in Brisbane before the Wet.'

'Maybe you're wise,' said Keitha. She wondered if she included her among those stupid females, and reflected that if she had any sense she would follow his example—though of course she knew she might have no choice. There was no doubt that the boss of Wayaway was a powerfully attractive male.

When the record ended, Mellie and Col went happily inside to put on another one. They at least appeared to be enjoying themselves. Bill and Keitha started dancing again, Dane strolled around from the side verandah, and presently there were two other couples on the floor. This time Justine, her cheeks flushed, danced with Col, and Mellie was where they all longed to be—in the boss's arms. But Mellie looked faintly bored.

Suddenly Keitha almost wanted to laugh. What a funny lot they were—herself very much included! *She* wanted to dance with Dane—yet wouldn't that only serve to bring her dismissal nearer? If he danced with her, he would want to talk about her going.

Yet, when he did dance with her, such depressing thoughts went clean out of her head. Because dancing with Dane was something she had dreamed about. He was more magnetically and sexually attractive than any man she had ever met. To be in his arms, to be so close to him, threw her mind into utter confusion. He was not a wonderfully proficient dancer. He interpreted the rhythm in his own way, lazily, almost mindlessly, so that it seemed to pulse through their two bodies.

After a long long time, Keitha managed to say, glancing up at him through dark lashes, 'I thought I was on your black list tonight—that you weren't going to dance with me.'

'Now why would you think that? It would have been inexcusable in a host, wouldn't it?' He looked down mockingly into her face. 'No, honey, there was a little matter I wanted to clear up with Justine first of all. And then you *were* rather occupied with the book-keeper, weren't you? ... But you're far from being on my black list. Remember I once called you a hibiscus flower? Well, a hibiscus bloom needs a light touch.

156

And I've been far from sure I could use a light touch when it comes to Keitha Godwin.'

She didn't know what he was talking about. It was like a riddle, but she couldn't drag her eyes from his. Her heart was hammering. Somehow they had drifted to the far end of the verandah where there was scarcely any light. They were barely moving, but stood close, locked together, his two arms holding her to him.

He asked softly, his sensuous mouth curving in a half-smile that might not be a smile at all, 'Are we going to talk about your love life in London?'

'I thought we were going to talk about my leaving Wayaway.' She felt herself trembling.

'Isn't it the same thing?'

There was a pause. She tried to sort herself out, but with his arms about her she could not think clearly at all. She wanted to say, 'My love life in London has ended,' but she could only shake her head.

'All right.' He sounded suddenly positive, even brisk. 'We'll forget London if that's how you want it. But watch out, honey—for in future there's going to be no more light handling.'

Suddenly they were dancing properly again, down towards the others at the lighted end of the verandah, and nothing had been resolved at all. And in next to no time, Kate came to tell them that supper was ready, and to remind them that it was a working day tomorrow.

Keitha finally went to bed feeling thoroughly restless and on edge. She tried to tell herself, 'I hate Dane Langley,' but she knew that she didn't and never would...

In the morning when she got up, Mellie, Col and Dane had already left the house, and Patty Drummond wore an air of smug satisfaction. Although she had insisted that Keitha would have to help with the household chores, Kate would not hear of it, saying that the housegirls were perfectly capable of coping and that Keitha must treat herself to a holiday. So she tidied her room after breakfast and finally found her way to the verandah. Justine was sitting there smoking and staring moodily out over the garden, and Keitha asked her, 'Aren't you going out to find the others?'

Justine's eyes narrowed. 'That's just what I'm not going to do. No, Keitha, as from now, I leave Dane strictly to Mellie. It appears that's what he wants.'

Keitha blinked. It seemed an extraordinary change of attitude. She asked curiously, 'What's happened?'

The clear grey-green eyes were turned towards her. 'Seeing you're only a visitor and don't belong here, I'll tell you something, Keitha. It's not all signed and settled yet, but Dane let me know pretty definitely last night that he's made up his mind who he's going to marry. It's Mellie, of course. No more playing around, was the way he put it. You might have noticed I was looking a bit dashed when we came in from the garden while you were dancing ... But shut up about it, won't you? We don't want to precipitate matters with a lot of talk.'

Keitha was staring at her. She felt all the colour drain from her face. So Mellie was to be the girl after all! Mellie had somehow made the grade. Lucky, lucky Mellie. All the life and energy seemed to drain out of her, she wanted to close her eyes and weep. Which was utterly ridiculous, because everyone had told her the boss had his eye on Mellie.

Justine was saying, 'This is why he's asked the Drummonds to stay, of course ... So you see now why I'm not running after them this morning. A girl has *some* pride. And strictly between us, Keitha, if I can manage it I intend to be nicely tied up myself before Dane drops his bombshell on the rest of the community. He's a heartless brute, when you come to think of it. Oh well——' She grimaced tiredly and reached for the cigarettes on a nearby table, lit one and squinted through smoke into brilliant sunlight. 'I'm not all that keen on the Gulf Country. How does it appeal to you?'

'I love it,' said Keitha without even having to think. Her heart ached. Soon—very soon—she would have to leave it.

'It's easy enough to love when you're just passing through,' commented Justine. 'For my part, I prefer the city. But for Dane, I'd never have come back to Tyrone Park. Even so, there are times when I look at those endless, endless plains—at that distant, distant horizon—or lie in bed listening to the empty, empty silence—and I don't think I can stand it another day.' She flicked Keitha a half rueful look. 'Well, I shan't have to now, shall I? Funny, isn't it? Col loves it, Mellie loves it—she couldn't wait to get back here after boarding school, not like me. To Dane, it's more than life. But I wish my father had done anything else in the world other than run a cattle station out here. If I'd never lived on Tyrone Park—never met Dane Langley—I'd have been perfectly happy in the city. Instead, it worked in me like a sickness. I forgot the everlasting plains and the dust and the heat, because I was haunted by a certain face—a certain man, who seemed like a god or something.' She laughed briefly. 'I guess I'm cured this time. You're lucky—safely in love with someone else, not likely to be caught up that way.'

Keitha listened confusedly. She was lucky—not caught up. How wrong Justine was! Wherever she went in the future she knew that a certain face would haunt her—the face of a man who called her honey, and was rough and tough and casual and cruel, and

159

certain that he was always right. A man who was heartless and was going to settle for a marriage that would be sensible for a cattleman—— She was by no means safely in love with someone else, and she wondered why Justine should think she was. And who did she mean?

Someone stepped up on to the verandah and the screen door shut with a bang that made Keitha jump.

'What's got into you two?' It was Bill Sutton. 'I've been expecting all morning to see you come pelting across the yard to saddle up your horses and chase out after the great white boss.'

'Well, that's just what we're not going to do this morning, Bill,' said Justine with a provocative smile.

Bill stared. 'I don't get it.' He looked at Keitha. 'How about coming out riding with me?'

'I'd like to,' said Keitha, who was hardly responsible at the moment for what she said.

Justine ashed her cigarette and stood up. 'I'm coming too,' she announced.

Bill gave her a long, hard, unrelenting look. Then, with a shrug—'All right. I'll see you both over in the saddling yard as soon as you're ready.'

The girls went off to change into jeans and shirts. Keitha was ready first and went to find Kate to tell her they were going riding with Bill.

'See you all stick together, then,' said Kate, who was busy sorting fresh vegetables on the kitchen table. 'And make sure you have a reliable mount—Dane wouldn't like you to take risks.'

'I'll take Summer,' said Keitha. She felt numb, as if her very heart had stopped beating. She knew she meant to get away from the others somehow, for like Justine she had some thinking to do.

When they reached the saddling yards, Summer had been saddled and a little black colt named Joe, as well as the horse Bill usually rode.

Justine took one look at the black colt and headed for Summer.

'I don't trust that little devil,' she told Bill.

'There's nothing wrong with Joe. Summer's Keitha's mount. Come on now, Justine—you're so wild about the outback. Keitha's a London girl.'

'I'm not the pioneering type,' Justine said with a smile. 'Maybe Keitha is.' As she spoke she swung herself gracefully and agilely into the saddle. 'Keitha loves the Gulf Country. She'll try anything—more tales to take home to her boy-friend when she leaves us.'

Her boy-friend. There it was again. Where did Justine get her information? Well, it didn't matter—none of it mattered now. Keitha looked at the little black horse. He was standing quietly and he didn't look a devil to her. She would sooner have had Summer, of course, but there was no question of that now. She put a hand gently on his neck and he eyed her mildly, and Bill crossed over and gave her a leg up into the saddle.

'Joe's all right. He doesn't like the spur, that's all, so just use your heels with caution and you'll be all right.'

A moment later they all trotted out of the yard, and Justine in the lead flung back over her shoulder, 'How much longer do you intend working out here, Bill?'

'I wouldn't have a notion,' said Bill, though it was not what he had told Keitha the night before. 'Why? Are you interested?'

'Not particularly. But I'm going back to Brisbane.' Justine touched her horse's flank and Summer broke into a gallop and was away across the plain. Bill followed, but Keitha's horse was suddenly fractious, pulling on the bit and tossing his head back, and prancing sideways. It was a minute or two before she had him under control and set off after the others who were by now some way ahead.

She didn't try to catch up with them, and looked for an excuse to leave them. She had the distinct impression that Justine would prefer it that way.

She allowed them to get a long way ahead of her, and presently they slowed down to a walk and moved along side by side. Obviously they were talking to each other, and Keitha had no intention of intruding and making a third. After a few minutes she galloped closer and called out, 'I think I'll go back. This horse and I don't agree terribly well.'

They both drew rein and turned round to wait for her.

'Yes, go and talk to Kate,' suggested Justine, obviously far from displeased at the idea of Keitha's leaving them.

But Bill said, 'Want me to come with you?'

'No, of course not. I'm all right. It's just I'm not really enjoying riding Joe.'

'Bill should have made a better choice,' said Justine. 'We'll see you at lunch, Keitha.'

'Right.'

She started back the way they had come, but she didn't intend going back to the homestead. She wanted to be by herself. She knew the track to the airstrip and thought she would go that way. Then no one could accuse her of trying to get lost or to create trouble making adventures for herself.

She let her horse amble along as slowly as it pleased, and she thought hard about what Justine had told her. So Dane Langley had made up his mind, had he? And he had kindly told Justine, and Justine—exactly as Col had said, though he had not been speaking of any specific girl—was now prepared to think again about Bill. Somehow Keitha did not think that Bill would make it easy for her. He was not the type to come meekly running when he was whistled.

And what about Mellie? Keitha wondered if Mellie had been told the verdict yet—if Patty was rejoicing. Wasn't Mellie supposed to *have* a mind of her own? Wasn't it even conceivable that given the chance she just might prefer Col? But then Mellie would be given no choice. 'That's not the way we do things out here.'

Keitha was working herself up to feel good and angry about the boss of Wayaway—who was so arrogant and domineering he could throw everyone around him into a turmoil. She found anger more bearable than heartbreak.

She had bypassed the homestead now and ridden almost to the airstrip. Before they reached the gate, she turned her horse's head and rode out towards a line of trees. Her mind went back to the conversation she had had with Dane the night before. What had he meant by saying that there was going to be no more light handling? Did he mean that her days at Wayaway were over, that he was going to pack her off at last? Well, she would get in first. She would ask to be taken to the outstation for the rest of her things, and she would take the next mail plane. That would show him how little she cared. It was a great pity she hadn't paid more attention to what Bill Sutton had told her weeks ago. She had thought then that she was impregnable. And she hadn't been, after all.

She was so deep in her thoughts that she had been paying almost no attention to where she was going. Dimly she was aware that there were trees—giant ant-hills—and now she had to lower her head or sway to one side every so often as they passed among the trees. Then suddenly a small branch nearby crashed down, her heart leaped and her muscles tensed, and she must have dug her heels into the black colt's sides. Either that or the falling branch startled him, for suddenly he seemed to go crazy, and raced hell-bent through the trees in a mad gallop.

Keitha was terrified. Sooner or later she was going to fall or to be swept from the saddle by one of those overhanging branches. All too soon she realised she simply hadn't the strength to control the horse in his present mood.

Then before the drastic thing she feared could happen, they were clear of the trees and pounding towards a steep creek bank. The perspiration was pouring down her back and her face felt cold and clammy. She tried desperately to check the maddened horse and then, exhausted, gave in. All she could do was to hang on and pray.

Seconds later, she heard the thundering of hooves behind. A horseman overtook her, riding in so close that before she knew what had happened he had shouldered her runaway mount around and in no time at all brought him to a halt. Keitha sat trembling and exhausted in the saddle.

Dane's voice—for of course it had to be Dane—exclaimed angrily, 'My God, you're a fool of a girl! Were you trying to kill yourself, galloping at the bank in such a murderous way?' He had swung out of the saddle and reached up to lift her to the ground. Her legs seemed to give way beneath her, and she relaxed against him.

CHAPTER TEN

She must have lapsed into momentary unconsciousness, for the next thing she knew, his voice came to her swimmingly through a ripple of yellow grass and dazzling sunlight.

'Here—drink this.'

She sipped, swallowed, and the fiery taste of brandy made her cough. She was half lying, half sitting against a tree trunk, and Dane's arm was about her shoulders. Nearby the two horses stood, their reins thrown over a branch.

'Honey,' Dane said, 'why do you do these things?' His face was very close to hers and those strange blue eyes seemed to look right into the depth of her being. There was neither anger nor laughter in them now, and for a long moment she felt she was confronted by the very essence of the man—deeply serious, vital, intense. She was like a needle being drawn to a magnet —slowly—inexorably——

She shuddered and pushed the flask away.

'I don't like anyone to be killed on my cattle run,' said Dane. 'Not anyone at all.' Still his eyes burned into hers, and she leaned back weakly against the strength of his arm. It was not until he moved to screw the cap on to the flask that she roused herself enough to say shakily, 'I should never *let* myself be killed on your cattle run, Dane Langley. I intend to walk off it under my own steam.'

'Do you indeed? And just when are you planning to do that?'

'When the Drummonds go back to the outstation.'

'Well, that won't be for quite a while yet,' he said

humouringly. That of course was because he wanted Mellie around—to compete his wooing. The memory made her rally.

'Then I'll go sooner. Just as soon as you like.'

'As soon as *I* like? Have I something to do with it, then?' That was unanswerable and she remained silent. 'In my opinion, it would be a pity for you to pull out. You've acclimatised so well, when I think back to that first day.' He smiled into her eyes, and she had to close them. It was like a knife in her heart. 'You stepped off that plane looking so much like the trendily dressed tourist come to take a look at the unthinkable outback. Since then——' He broke off and took a packet of cigarettes from his pocket, lit two, and gave her one. Though she seldom smoked, she took it. She needed something to steady her nerves just now, as he lounged beside her in the shade of the trees, his eyes narrowed against the glare from the plains.

Watching him through her lashes, she found herself thinking, 'I'll have this to remember—and it will be something and yet nothing.' It was both pain and pleasure simply to look at him—his jutting chin, his sunbleached hair, his deeply tanned face...

He turned his head suddenly and caught her out staring, and she felt the colour rush into her pale cheeks. His lips curved in that enigmatic suggestion of a smile.

'I've never yet persuaded you to talk about London, have I? Well, I warned you last night that I was finished with using a light touch. And now I've got you lying here, full of brandy and scared stiff, all the fight gone out of you, I'm going to really outdo myself and twist your arm until you give.'

She stared at him fascinated, put the cigarette to her lips and drew on it—saw the trembling of her hand.

'My private life is my own concern,' she said shakily.

'Is it?' His eyes were quizzical. 'Isn't this a sort of private life, though—you and me lying here together in the midday heat, alone in the world? Doesn't it seem fateful, too, that I called in at the homestead to pick you up and thereby arrived here just at the right moment to save your life?'

Was there a tinge of irony in his voice? Was he—playing her along? She said defensively, 'I'm sorry, but I don't *really* think you saved my life. I got through that belt of trees without an accident. I might have taken a tumble in the creek, but I don't think I'd have been killed.'

'No one ever thinks they're going to be killed, honey. But I tell you I was really afraid what was going to happen to you.'

'And you weren't ready for it—because you hadn't heard the story of my life?' She was trying hard to be flippant because she was somehow frightened of him in his present mood.

'Something like that,' he agreed nonchalantly. His face came closer to hers. One hand took hold of hers that was holding the cigarette and pressed it hard against the hardness of the ground. The other pulled her to him—even harder—and his lips were against hers . . .

Despite herself, despite what Justine had told her about Mellie, she felt herself surrendering, going limp . . . With a sudden effort, she pushed him away, and drew back breathing quickly.

'How can you do that when——'

'When you're all but passing out? When you haven't got over the fright you gave yourself just now? Frankly, honey, I think there couldn't be a better time. I told you I was going to twist your arm. I've got you at my mercy now—I can find out things I wouldn't find out if you had all your wits about you and all your usual defences in position.'

'What kind of things?' She hadn't even meant to ask the question.

He gave a deep-throated laugh. 'Come on, honey— admit that you're rather more than attracted to me. You did give yourself away pretty thoroughly just now, you know.'

She refused to answer his eyes, half-closed her own and stared at the ground. She saw an ant move, this way, then turn back; hesitate, move on again. Then back once more. 'That's like me,' she thought miserably. And she thought of Mellie, and wished she could hate him too.

He said gently, 'All right, I'll make the first move. I'm very much—maybe too much—attracted to you, Keitha. It happened right at the beginning, over at the coast.'

Her eyes flicked up warily and she looked straight into blue fire. The book-keeper had said, 'He'll play you along—if that's what you want. But there'll be nothing in it for you.' She bit her lip hard and looked away from him.

He drew a sharp impatient breath. 'You tantalising, maddening, tormenting girl! Let's get to the bottom of all this. Are you—or are you not—going back to England?'

'I—I don't know,' she said desperately.

'Then listen to me, honey. You'd better damn well make up your mind. What's the strength of all this talk about you over the galah sessions?'

That drew her glance again. 'What talk?' she asked sharply. She thought suddenly of the locked office door at the outstation—of Patty Drummond's refusal to let her join in the talk with the women from other cattle runs. She thought of the one day when she had chattered rather freely to Patty about Donn Gorsky ...

'*What* talk?' she repeated.

'Don't you know? Honey, it's all over the Gulf that you've a man waiting for you in London—that you'll be married as soon as you get back. Well, I calculate you don't act like a girl in love, but there are all those letters to think about. And remember the night you called me Donn?'

Colour flooded her face, then drained away again. She felt furious with Patty Drummond for talking about her, for being so indiscreet. But of course it had been done deliberately. It explained why Justine O'Boyle had said, 'You're safely in love with someone else.' Well, it was not true. She was not going back to London to be married. Yet why tell Dane that? He was going to marry Mellie Drummond, he had no right to be kissing Keitha Godwin out here under the trees.

Troubled, she stared out at the line of trees that marked the steep river bank, at the shadows that fell across the long grasses, at the distant line where sky met land and a heat haze shimmered and danced.

His voice cut through her thoughts with whip-like cruelty. 'Come on now, let's have it. Are you going to marry him?'

For the life of her, she couldn't tell the direct lie. There was a long pause. He waited relentlessly.

She said at last, her voice low, 'There's never been anything definite. I——'

His eyes narrowed, the pupils were pinpoints of blackness. 'Well, that's an admission of some sort. But what a time it's taken to get it out of you! That kiss we shared just now—that wasn't merely a friendly kiss on either side, was it? ... Right, we'll take it from there. The inquisition's over.' He gave her a dark look, and there was a glint away back in his eyes that she couldn't fathom.

Her head was spinning, and it was not the brandy.

What did he mean when he said, 'We'll take it from there?'—when he commented on that more than passionate kiss? Hadn't he told Justine only last night, 'No more playing around?'

She said, groping for caution, for sense, for escape from the utter madness that was ready to swallow her up, 'Correction, Dane. The inquisition's not *quite* over. I have a question. What about Mellie?'

'Mellie?' The sunbleached eyebrows went up. 'My God, must we always come back to Mellie? What about her?'

'You're—you're going to marry her, aren't you?'

'Have you been listening to Patty Drummond? ... No, I am not going to marry Mellie.'

Keitha blinked. 'But Justine said——' She stopped. Justine had said to 'shut up' about that. She said instead, 'Does Mellie know? Have you—told her?'

The brows came down darkly now. 'What do you take me for? Mellie's been brought up from childhood with the idea that if she plays her cards right she'll finish up being Mrs Dane Langley. She hasn't got beyond that yet—not quite. But she will. One day she'll find out for herself what love is all about, and that day she'll have grown up. But she's got to do it on her own—I'm not going to push her. I can only continue to treat her gently.' He stopped. Keitha's mouth had opened in protest, and his lips quirked. 'All right. Except on the odd occasion when I find her chasing calves and dicing with death.' He stood up and reached down a hand to her. 'And now I think we'd better get you home. How do you feel about getting back on to that black colt?'

Keitha looked at Joe. 'I can manage,' she said firmly.

'That's my girl!' Her hand was still in his hand and he pulled her against him and his lips came down on hers in a kiss that was all fierceness and passion.

At last, weakly, she broke free. 'Please, Dane——'

He grinned down at her. 'Hardly the time or the place, is it? I agree. Come on, let's get going.'

They rode back to the homestead together and Keitha felt oddly happy. But it was a shaky, precarious kind of happiness, a happiness that she could not trust.

The following days reminded her of her first week on Wayaway, when Dane had taken her out on the run with him every day. But this time Mellie was always there too, and Dane was so soft with Mellie, so gentle and affectionate that Keitha could feel the poison of jealousy eating into her in spite of what he had told her. She could not help seeing herself as an intruder who had pushed her way into the life on the Wayaway cattle run and was trying to disrupt the ordered pattern of events.

Her new relationship with Dane had not crystallised. She still had no real idea where she stood with him except that he found her perhaps disturbingly physically attractive. Hadn't he at the very beginning called her a 'sexy, trendily dressed girl'? Perhaps he was looking for no more than a light affair—like the one he had had with Justine.

Justine, despite Dane's rejection of her, was in no hurry to return to Tyrone Park. Pretty, poised, and unruffled as ever, she still teased and provoked the boss of Wayaway, though Keitha often thought she could detect a touch of barely concealed malice in her banter. She never came out riding with them, and Keitha knew she was concentrating all her attention on the book-keeper. What progress she was making was uncertain. Keitha had an idea that Bill would make it hard for her, if he played along with her at all. He was not a soft or forgiving sort of man by any manner of means. If Justine had decided she would be happy with him, she would have to fight for him and to forget her pride pretty thoroughly. Otherwise she would have small hope of getting herself 'well and truly tied up' before Dane dropped the bombshell she at least expected him to drop.

One thing was for sure: those who loved Dane Langley and lost had it hard...

As in Keitha's first week on Wayaway, Dane went out early, then came back for her later on. Sometimes Mellie went with him at sunup, sometimes she waited with Keitha. But always Patty Drummond was hovering in the background, cold, disapproving, hostile towards Keitha, full of orders and instructions for her daughter.

There was something a little sad and desperate about Mellie these days. Much of her bounce and vitality had gone and she had a vaguely lost air. Even when there was work to be done with the cattle, and she was in the thick of it, she seemed always conscious of Dane's critical eye upon her, and fearful that she would invoke his displeasure. It was hard to remember that she had ever defied him—said she hated him.

All during that week the mobs that had been mustered on various parts of the run for the sales were being brought into the holding paddock near the homestead, and the size of the mob there was growing and growing. One evening as they rode home behind the cattle, and Mellie was somewhere ahead hidden in the sunstruck haze of red dust, Dane remarked, 'Mellie's like a bee in a bottle just now. I'd like to know how much longer it's going to take her to wake up to herself and discover what it is that ails her. Right now, she thinks her world's in pieces because it looks very much like the boss of Wayaway isn't going to marry her. Yet that's not really Mellie's trouble at all.' He glanced over at Keitha who rode beside him and his eyes had a thoughtful look.

Keitha wanted to ask, 'What *is* Mellie's trouble?' but she was terribly afraid that Dane was wrong and that Mellie was in love with him and eating her heart out. Mellie tried so hard to please him these days, and it could not be doubted that she would make a wonderful wife for a cattleman, even if Justine thought her too unsophisticated.

This evening the sky on the far horizon was covering over with cloud, and there were rumblings of distant thunder. Vivid streaks of lightning spilt dramatically through dark purple clouds and Keitha felt restlessly that these threatening storms seemed to heighten the general tension. The Wet was still weeks away, but soon there would be stars in the evenings. Dane had said that morning that Justine must go back to Tyrone Park before one or two heavy falls made the rivers impassable. There was always the chance of that happening and then they would be isolated at Wayaway in their little closed community.

When they reached the homestead that evening, Justine had gone. The book-keeper had taken her, Kate said, and he would stay away overnight and return the following day.

'That girl should go back to city life,' Patty Drummond remarked complacently at dinner. 'She doesn't really belong out here.'

Keitha caught Dane's satirical glance across the dining room table. Someone—Kate or Patty—had put candles on the table. The women were dressed up— Patty always dressed for dinner, because she had good clothes, designed and made by herself, and she liked to wear them; Kate dressed because she always had and it was habit; Mellie dressed up because her mother nagged and nagged at her until she had to change for sheer peace of mind. And Keitha—Keitha got into her pretty, dressy clothes simply because she wanted Dane to like the look of her.

Now he said laconically, 'What Justine does is up to her. You're too fond of ordering people's lives for them, Patty.'

Patty looked down at her plate to hide her expression, and Keitha wanted to laugh. She thought she knew what Patty would have liked to say! Dane was something of an expert at ordering people's lives for them too. Instead, Patty said coldly, 'Not at all, Dane. You know perfectly well that all of us do just as *you* decree.'

'Well, that's how it should be,' he said equably. 'Another glass of wine, Kate?' He reached for the bottle and poured it. 'Ask Kate. She's submitted to my father—and to me—for a good part of her life and she's never regretted it. As for you, Patty, d'you think I made a mistake—insisting you stay on at the outstation?'

'Sometimes I do think that, Dane,' said Patty a little bitterly. 'Sometimes I wonder *why* you asked us to stay on.'

'One of these days,' said Dane, 'when Mellie's a little bit older and wiser, you'll know why, Patty. Meanwhile, if you don't want to stay, you're free to go to the coast. You've always been free.'

Mellie, who was staring down at her lap, suddenly raised her head and burst out into the momentary silence, 'I'd die at the coast! I'd hate it!'

'That's what I thought,' said Dane. 'What are we going to do with you, Mellie? We'll have to marry you off to someone who's as much in love with the Gulf Country as you are yourself. Which reminds me—I was going to suggest you go back to the outstation tomorrow, after the mail's come. It's pretty lonely there for Col, and he'll be here in the afternoon.'

Patty tossed her head. 'It's lonelier for me, Dane.'

'I thought you'd changed your mind about that,' he mocked. 'And you can take Keitha with you, you know.'

Patty fingered her wine glass and looked coldly across the table at the pale-faced slender girl whose eyes were deeply shadowed in the candlelight. Her dislike was plain. 'Keitha will be leaving us soon. She has ties—commitments—in England.'

'She has an aunt,' said Dane mildly.

'And a man friend,' flashed Patty. 'Perhaps she hasn't told you that.' She turned to Keitha, her look intense. 'Didn't you tell me that the man you worked for at the television studio is in love with you—that you were in love with him?'

'I suppose I did,' said Keitha slowly. She had flushed crimson and would have given anything on earth to be able to have that conversation unsaid.

There was a hard light in Dane's eyes. 'Keitha's not in a hurry to go.'

'Oh, really, Dane,' Patty snapped. 'You can't possibly think she would change the excitement of her life in London for our little backwater, that would be too much to believe.'

If only Dane would ask *her* that question, Keitha thought. She knew very well what her answer would be. But Dane didn't ask her.

Later that night, while they were all sitting on the verandah, she went out to the kitchen to make coffee. Before taking it out to the others, she slipped into her room for the magazine she had been reading. It had an article in it that Kate wanted. She didn't bother putting the light on, and as she moved across the room she heard Patty's voice saying her name.

'I don't need her any longer, Dane, and if you must know, we don't get on. You'd be doing me a favour if you put her on the plane tomorrow. After all, she'll want to see something of her brother before she goes back to England to be married.'

Keitha was about to switch on the light to warn them that she was there, but now she paused. What did Dane believe? She had told him she had no such plans. Did he believe her or Patty?

In a moment his voice came drawlingly. 'Now, Patty, you've built on to what the girl told you to suit yourself.'

'Indeed I've done no such thing! If you knew how many letters she writes—how many she gets from that man—— You're blind, Dane, if you think there's nothing in it. Of course she wants to have a good time while she's out here—and an engaged girl isn't likely to get that. She's enjoyed herself flirting with Colin—with Bill—and of course she'd like to flirt with you.'

Keitha's blood boiled. She had listened too long. She flicked on the light and the voices receded.

When she woke the next morning she heard the bellowing of cattle in the holding yards. Soon the mob of nine hundred beasts would be on the road, soon the Wet would come, soon the Drummonds would depart for the outstation. Everything was going to happen at once, yet nothing—nothing—happened to her, Keitha Godwin. It was as if Dane were playing a cruel game with her that had no ending. It was mail day, and she tried to distract herself wondering if—and what—she would hear from Martin. she was half expecting that he and Julie Warner were announcing their engagement. That would mean a link between the Godwins and, indirectly, the Langleys. Which brought her, maddeningly, back to Dane.

She jumped out of bed and went to the doors that opened on to the verandah. The day looked exactly the same as any other. Bright sunlight filtered through the crimson flowers of the bougainvillea, the mango trees were motionless, their leaves unmoved by even the slightest breeze, and the faint nostalgic scent of the oleanders drifted about the verandah.

Justine had gone. That was the only difference in the day. And that meant exactly nothing, because it was some days since she had been vitally concerned with Dane Langley. He had told her he had made up his mind who he would marry. And he had told Keitha it was not Mellie. Then who was it? Keitha decided she would be a fool if she took anything for granted.

Her nerves were stretched taut, she was edgy, distracted, uncertain, beginning to feel that she had been mad to allow herself to fall in love with Dane. The whole situation was becoming subtly intolerable. Something was going to have to happen to break the tension.

And yet today was exactly like any other day.

She showered, got into her jeans, and went out to breakfast. Dane and Mellie had gone already, Patty was still in bed, and there were only herself and Kate at the end of the verandah.

Keitha said, pouring black coffee, 'I never did settle with you about those paintings, Kate. I'd like to send one to England in time for Christmas. And of course I should like one for myself.'

'Why the hurry?' asked Kate, with her friendly smile. 'But if you like, we'll get something sorted out this morning after I've got things organised in the kitchen.'

Dane arrived before she had come back from the kitchen. He found Keitha waiting on the verandah, her hat under her chair.

'Do you want to come out today or have you had enough? I'll be back in time to meet the mail plane, if you prefer to have a lazy morning. You look tired.'

She didn't want a lazy morning. If she looked tired it was because her thoughts of him had kept her awake. Didn't he know yet how she loved the run—the dust and the cattle and, more than anything else, riding at his side? She stood up unhurriedly. 'I must have my exercise.'

He gave her an odd look. 'Exercise! Is that all it is?' She flushed deeply and refused to look at him. 'Well, hang on for a minute—I want to remind Kate that Col will be here later on. We've plans to check over to get the mob on the road.'

'All this will be over soon, won't it? Once you've got your cattle moving——'

'Yes. Then in no time we'll have the Wet, and we can all take it easy.' He disappeared in the direction of the kitchen and she stood waiting, looking pensively out into the sunlit garden. When he came back she asked, as they headed for the saddling yard, 'What will you do during the Wet, Dane?'

'Well, that rather depends,' he said guardedly. 'I usually go over to the coast.'

'And the Drummonds?'

He shrugged. 'They come along too.'

'So there'll be no job for me at the outstation.'

'That's right.' He smiled at her in an intimate way that made her heart thud. They both knew that there was no job for her at the outstation already . . .

He saw her mounted, swung himself into the saddle, and they were off . . .

She came back with him after lunch. Mellie was somewhere behind with the stockmen. Keitha wondered vaguely if she would hear Donn's reaction to her letter when the mail came in. She didn't particularly care one way or the other. Donn had faded very much into a background figure. She hoped she had done the

same as far as he was concerned. He was always involved with a number of people—both men and women. One thing was certain—he would never lack for
admirers, and being Donn, even if he thought Keitha
had broken his heart, he would soon be circulating
freely again.

They left their horses in the yard and Dane looked
back frowningly.

'Mellie's taking her time.'

His arm was across Keitha's shoulders as they went
towards the garden, and she remembered how once she
had told him she didn't like to be touched. Now—his
arm laid across her shoulders was like the kiss of life ...

In the garden Patty, wearing a wide-brimmed cotton
hat and green gardening gloves, was watering some
small plants.

'Wait till I tell you the news,' she said as they drew
near. She turned the stream of water aside and they
both stopped. 'It came over the radio transceiver on
the morning schedule.' Her eyes were bright and mali-
cious, and for some reason Keitha's heart began to
pound.

'Yes?' said Dane. His arm was now around Keitha's
waist, and the girl saw Patty's glance flick there and
back.

'Justine O'Boyle and Bill Sutton have decided to get
married.'

Dane looked really surprised. He obviously hadn't a
notion that this was an old affair come back to life, or
that he had ever been the cause of obstructing it.

'Well, what do you know! I thought Justine came to
see me! Is Bill going to work on Tyrone Park?'

'Dear me, no. They're moving to Brisbane. They
mean to get away before the Wet, and they'll be
married at the coast.'

'Well, that's fine. I knew we were going to have to

find a new book-keeper. Bill misses the life of the city.'

They started to move on. Patty said, her voice cracking, 'Oh, Keitha, there's a message for you in your room. Something you've been waiting for, I think.'

Keitha's nerves jumped. Was it to do with leaving the outstation? Surely Patty was not giving her formal notice——

They had reached the verandah steps when Patty called Dane back. 'There's something I wanted to tell you, Dane.'

He went back, and Keitha went on, still wondering about that message.

When she reached her room she threw her hat on the bed and crossed to the dressing table where she saw a folded sheet of paper. She opened it out.

Carefully written out in Kate's handwriting was a telegram that had been relayed over the morning schedule. It said simply, 'You win. Come home and we'll be married with all the trimmings. Love—Donn.'

CHAPTER ELEVEN

SHE read it twice, feeling somehow shocked, aware that it was public property. It was what she had wanted— long, long ago, it seemed. Now it meant nothing at all. She stood at the dressing table, the message in her hands, and looked up to meet her own eyes, dark and troubled, in the mirror. For the first time, she felt for Donn—really felt for him. Yet hadn't he taken her letter rather lightly? He had thought he had only to use the magic word 'married' and she would come running back to him.

'No, Donn,' she thought. 'You're much too late. I could never marry you now, no matter what happens.' It amazed her that he did not know it—that he didn't sense that this ephemeral thing between them had dissolved—vanished. It had never been based on a real understanding. Otherwise, he could never have even suggested that she should shack up with him.

She heard footsteps coming round the verandah, and then Dane stood at the door, hands low on his hips, bleached hair ruffled, brows down, eyes flashing fire. On his mouth that half smile that was not a smile at all.

'So you've got what you were waiting for, have you? It's all definite enough now, I take it, Keitha Godwin. You'd better pack your things and I'll put you on the plane. One thing I'd like to say—I don't appreciate being used in a battle of tactics.'

Keitha stared at him appalled. She understood perfectly that Patty Drummond had told him what was in that telegram, and had given her own interpretation of it.

'You don't understand,' she said confusedly, hardly knowing where to begin. 'I wrote to Donn—I told him——'

And at that fateful moment there was an interruption. It was Kate, too urgent for ceremony.

'Dane, Mellie's been thrown from her horse. One of the stockmen's come in. He didn't like to move her. You'll have to drive out at once——'

He swung round, eyes alert, watchful. 'Where is she?'

'Mick will show you—he's waiting outside.'

He paused for a second at the door to say, his voice hard and impersonal, 'Kate, see that Keitha gets packed up. She's going on the plane this afternoon.'

Then he was gone.

Keitha looked at Kate. She felt dizzy, stricken, her face was white. 'Mellie—is it bad?'

'I hope not. Dane will take Patty along. We'll soon know.' She looked at Keitha, her eyes puzzled. 'You're going? You mean to marry this man in England? I never believed it was true——'

Keitha, who had felt numb, now wanted to weep. She sat down abruptly on the side of the bed. The sheet of paper was still in her hands, and she stared at it blankly. 'No. Of course I'm not going to marry him.' She looked up at Kate. 'Dane doesn't understand. Perhaps he doesn't want to understand,' she went on hopelessly. 'Perhaps none of it matters.' She stood up and went mechanically to the wardrobe. Her eyes were blinded by tears, but she began to take down the dresses she had chosen with such care. She put her suitcase on the bed and began to fold her clothes carefully. It was all too much. The telegram—the misunderstanding—Mellie——

Behind her, Kate, who could not see the tears running down her cheeks, said gently, 'Tell me about it, Keitha.'

The girl wiped her eyes quickly and turned with a bright smile. 'Donn never wanted me to marry him before. We were in love—in a way—but he was in favour of one of those casual arrangements. It didn't suit me. And I didn't care any more after a while—I knew I would never go back and I wrote and told him. So then—after all that—he changed his mind about us——'

'Men!' said Kate. 'They think they can mend things in a minute—be forgiven anything.' She put a hand on Keitha's arm. 'Don't pack your clothes. You must tell Dane——'

'What's the use? I'd have to go sooner or later.'

Kate looked at her and shook her head. 'Do you *want* to go? Do you *want* to leave Wayaway—and Dane?'

Keitha bit her lip. The tears were coming again. 'I love it here,' she said shakily. 'More than anywhere on earth. But I was a fool ever to imagine—— And now this accident's happened, Dane will see it's Mellie he cares for.'

'Rubbish,' said Kate briskly. 'Mellie's never been more to Dane than a little sister, though Patty is too stubborn to accept it. I've never known him really in love until he met you.' Keitha gasped. What was Kate saying? Kate smiled a little. 'Then that silly woman spread those stories over the radio transmitter and of course everyone heard them, Dane heard them—that's why he tried to keep away from you, I could see that ... No, you mustn't go. You put your clothes away again, Keitha, and in a minute I'll have a pot of tea made. Patty will need a cup when she comes home. You need one now.'

'But Dane said——' began Keitha weakly.

'Never mind what Dane said.' It was the first time Keitha had ever heard Kate defy the boss, and now she was quite determined about it. 'You do as *I* say this time.'

Keitha abandoned her packing. Her thoughts were whirling. How would Kate know what went on in Dane Langley's mind? Yet Kate *would* know—he was the sun in her sky and she would make it her business to know and to understand ... She dried her tears and her thoughts returned to Mellie—big beautiful healthy Mellie, who wasn't yet really grown up. It was inconceivable that anything should have happened to Mellie.

Twenty minutes later the Land-Rover was back. By that time Keitha and Kate were drinking tea on the verandah, saying little, waiting, and thinking of Mellie. Dane came up the steps carrying the girl who was limp in his arms, her red hair hanging down. Patty, close behind them, looked sick. She was only too glad for Kate to take control, help her to a chair and hand her a cup of strong black tea. Dane had gone through into the sitting room and deposited Mellie on one of the couches. Keitha, without thinking, followed him and waited mutely. When he spoke, Kate was behind her listening too.

'No bones broken. I've already made sure of that. She's knocked herself out, probably got a bit of concussion. We'll have a word with the doc this afternoon over the transceiver. But I don't think there's anything to worry about.' He smiled grimly. 'She was after a calf, of course. But even when it comes to being thrown by a horse in dangerous circumstances it seems Mellie knows how to fall. Though she mightn't be so lucky next time.'

Kate looked tenderly at the girl who lay unconscious in the room. 'I'm glad she's all right. I'll slip back to

Patty now.'

Someone else came into the room then, tiptoeing clumsily in his stockmen's boots. It was Col, and he went straight to the couch where Mellie lay.

'Is she all right? I just got in. Patty says she's had a fall.'

'She's right as rain,' said Dane. His smile was gentle and reassuring. Col looked almost as green as Patty.

At that moment Mellie moaned—moved—opened her eyes. The two men stood looking down at her and her eyes went to them both—dazedly at first, and then with dawning recognition. But it was on Col's face that her glance stayed and suddenly she began to cry.

'Oh, Col—Col——' She put her fists to her face in a childish gesture.

Keitha saw Col and the boss exchange one brief telling look. There were tears in her own eyes and she didn't really know what passed between them. But something had. Some minute but subtle signal had been given and received, and in an instant Col was on his knees beside Mellie, soothing her, murmuring to her, her hand in his.

Dane turned away and went silently out to the verandah, and Keitha followed.

Once they had left the cool shadowy room behind them, his manner changed abruptly.

'Ready?' His voice was curt.

Keitha shook her head helplessly. Along the verandah there was now only Kate. Patty must have gone to her room, leaving her daughter to the care of those who could stand the sight of pain and hurt. Kate came towards them.

'I'll look after Mellie now, Dane. Is she conscious?'

'Just about. Better get her into bed presently. But leave her with Col for a minute or two. There's nothing much wrong with her. She's knocked herself out, and probably given herself a bit of a fright. Col too.' His mouth twisted in a faintly sardonic grin.

'Thank God it's no worse,' said Kate. 'You have a cup of tea, Dane. Then you've the plane to meet. Keitha might like to go out with you for the run.'

He stared at her. 'I told you to see she got packed up,' he blazed.

'I know you did, Dane. But she's not leaving.'

'She damn well is. I'm the one who gives the orders here——'

'Dane,' Kate broke in, 'I must go and see to Mellie. I'm not going to argue with you. Keitha will explain.'

Keitha didn't know that she wanted to explain. The boss of Wayaway was white about the nostrils. She had never before seen him in such a fury, and it was all waiting to descend on her head—even though she had done absolutely nothing to deserve it. When those fire blue eyes were turned on her behind Kate's departing back, she said with dignity, 'I'll pack—if that's what you want, Dane.'

'Surely it's what you must want too,' he retorted coldly.

'Is it? Then if you say so, it must be right.' She went quickly, head up, in the direction of her bedroom, and he followed her.

He lounged against the bedroom door while she bundled her clothes unceremoniously and rather angrily into the suitcase. He was puzzled, watchful; silent now. 'I still have some things at the outstation, Dane.'

'They'll be sent on.'

Silence again until she had snapped shut the lid of her suitcase. Then she raised her head and looked at him. She was debating with herself whether or not she should say anything about that telegram. If only she knew whether Kate was right! She said, with a cool

186

smile, 'Mellie's sorted herself out, hasn't she? I'm glad about that. Col is very much in love with Mellie. Do you suppose Patty will mind? And Justine—I hope she'll be happy with Bill——'

He was tapping impatiently against the door frame with the knuckles of one hand. Then he said with a savage movement, 'Mellie—Justine—all this evasion. What about you, Keitha Godwin? Kate said you'd explain. Have *you* sorted yourself out?'

'I sorted myself out long ago.' She turned away and began opening and closing drawers to make sure she had missed nothing. But the fact was, she couldn't go on looking at him without giving herself away.

But it was no use. A quick movement and he was behind her—had seized her shoulders in a painful grip, twisted her round so that she faced him helplessly. His eyes blazed down at her.

'It's time you gave me a full and proper explanation of a lot of things,' he said from between clenched teeth. His fingers bit into her flesh cruelly. 'I've asked you already God knows how many times——'

'You'll be late for the mail plane,' she breathed.

'So I'll be late for the mail plane. So it can wait for once—or take off or do what it damn well pleases. But we're neither of us budging from this room until you've told me exactly what you mean by that statement.'

'That I've sorted myself out?' Despite herself she was bristling with antagonism. How dared he ask her to state her position first! She looked him straight in the eye and thought she would die for the pain and pleasure of it, and she said distinctly, 'It's hardly your business. I'm not aware that it ever was. The position seems to be that you're throwing me out—which you've wanted to do since my very first week here. Well, now you're to have your wish—I'm going——'

187

'You implied that you didn't want to pack——'

'You're the boss, aren't you?' she said with irony.

He made an infuriated exclamation. 'This news you were waiting for—this proposal from that fellow in England——'

'That comes under the heading of private business too,' she said stubbornly. Why should she explain? She didn't have any sort of a proposal from *him*!

There was a long silence. Her heart had begun to beat fast. He was staring at her, waiting. It was a battle of wills; his attitude was an uncompromising and dogmatic 'Please explain'; hers was a stubborn, 'Tell me what *you* want first—and risk a rebuff'.

Then suddenly—unexpectedly—she knew she was going to give in. He was the stronger and she liked it that way. It had been different with Donn.

She sighed, and her lashes fell.

'Of course I'm not going to marry Donn.'

'Why not?' He was relentless.

'Because I don't love him.'

'Do you love—me? Come on now, this isn't the time to be putting on your bush orchid act. Put your head up and look at me. And for God's sake don't tell me it's none of my business.'

She looked up and he was laughing at her, but away back in his eyes was that dark intensity she had seen once before—the day her horse got out of control. She opened her mouth to say 'Yes—yes—of course I love you', but before she could say it, his lips were on hers.

A breathless moment went by, and then he let her go and said with satisfaction, 'Of course you love me. Now come on—or we'll miss that plane.'

She heard herself gasp, and he laughed again. 'Little idiot! What do you think I mean? ... Leave your stuff alone. But I've got to meet that plane and there are things you and I have to say to each other, honey, that

188

can't possibly wait till I get back.' He had her fast by the hand and she almost ran out of the room with him—along the verandah and down the three shallow steps, the screen door banging behind them.

She was breathing fast when they reached the Land-Rover, and in five seconds they were off.

'Are you sure Mellie will be all right, Dane?'

'Of course I'm sure. Besides, Col's there to look after her. Kate's there—Patty's there—though *she* won't be much use, as both you and I know.' He sent her a quick laughing look. 'Col's in heaven, Patty will be like a bear with a sore head—on two counts—and now you and I can forget the lot of them and think about ourselves. When are you going to marry me?'

She blinked and caught her breath. He was a fast worker!

He said musingly, 'Once the Wet's here, there's nothing much can be done on Wayaway. We'll go over to the coast and make our plans from there. You'll want to tell your brother, of course ... What do you say to Townsville for the wedding? Or would you sooner Brisbane? And a honeymoon in New Zealand? Or do you prefer Fiji?'

'Anywhere at all,' said Keitha blithely. 'Just whatever you say, Dane.'

He laughed softly and reached out to take her hand for a second.

'It's taken me longer than I've liked, Keitha Godwin, to make you say yes—to make you decide you care about my opinions after all.'

They could see the plane coming down now, and the Rover roared along the track in a cloud of dust and finally pulled up on the airstrip with perfect timing.

'We'll start spreading the news right away,' decided Dane, as they walked the few feet to the aircraft, his arm about her waist. The rear door opened, the pleasant young freight officer appeared, the steps were down.

'Hi, Dane—how're things?' He looked at Keitha with friendly curiosity. 'I reckon you must be enjoying yourself on Wayaway, Miss Godwin. You've been here quite a few weeks now.'

'She's enjoying herself so well I've persuaded her to stay on for good,' said Dane with a grin. 'And you have my permission to pass on that news to anyone and everyone. In fact,' he added, pulling Keitha possessively close,' we shall be very disappointed if it doesn't come back to us over the galah session this afternoon. Shan't we, honey?'

Keitha, aware that they were being watched from the plane by several pairs of interested eyes, felt suddenly shy and could only nod. Truth to tell, she was just a little bit afraid of her happiness yet. She waited while the freight and the mail were dealt with and was not satisfied until Dane's arm was about her again.

Then, looking up into the strength of his face, she wondered how she could possibly be scared of anything ever again if she was loved by the boss of Wayaway.

He was grinning down at her.

'Honey, don't look at me like that in a public place! Wait till that mail plane's gone—and then I'll be ready for anything!'

GOLDEN HARLEQUIN LIBRARY

A Treasury of Harlequin Romances!

Many of the all time favorite Harlequin Romance Novels have not been available, until now, since the original printing. But on this special introductory offer, they are yours in an exquisitely bound, rich gold hardcover with royal blue imprint. Three complete unabridged novels in each volume. And the cost is so very low you'll be amazed!

Golden Harlequin Library

Handsome, Hardcover Library Editions at Paperback Prices! ONLY $1.75 each volume.

This very special collection of 30 volumes (there'll be more!) of classic Harlequin Romances would be a distinctive addition to your library. And imagine what a delightful gift they'd make for any Harlequin reader!

Start your collection now. See reverse of this page for full details.

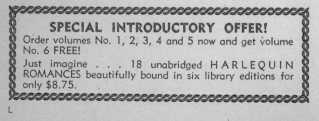

SPECIAL INTRODUCTORY OFFER!

Order volumes No. 1, 2, 3, 4 and 5 now and get volume No. 6 FREE!

Just imagine . . . 18 unabridged HARLEQUIN ROMANCES beautifully bound in six library editions for only $8.75.

L

GOLDEN HARLEQUIN LIBRARY — $1.75 each volume

Special Introductory Offer

(First 6 volumes only $8.75)

☐ **VOLUME I**
692 THE ONLY CHARITY, Sara Seale
785 THE SURGEON'S MARRIAGE
    Kathryn Blair
806 THE GOLDEN PEAKS
    Eleanor Farnes

☐ **VOLUME II**
649 KATE OF OUTPATIENTS
    Elizabeth Gilzean
774 HEATHERLEIGH, Essie Summers
853 SUGAR ISLAND, Jean S. Macleod

☐ **VOLUME III**
506 QUEEN'S COUNSEL, Alex Stuart
760 FAIR HORIZON, Rosalind Brett
801 DESERT NURSE, Jane Arbor

☐ **VOLUME IV**
501 DO SOMETHING DANGEROUS
    Elizabeth Hoy
816 THE YOUNGEST BRIDESMAID
    Sara Seale
875 DOCTOR DAVID ADVISES
    Hilary Wilde

☐ **VOLUME V**
721 SHIP'S SURGEON, Celine Conway
862 MOON OVER THE ALPS
    Essie Summers
887 LAKE OF SHADOWS, Jane Arbor

☐ **VOLUME VI**
644 NEVER TO LOVE, Anne Weale
650 THE GOLDEN ROSE, Kathryn Blair
814 A LONG WAY FROM HOME
    Jane Fraser

Just Published

($1.75 per volume)

☐ **VOLUME XXV**
531 DOCTOR MEMSAHIB, Juliet Shore
617 AND BE THY LOVE, Rose Burghley
680 BLACK CHARLES,
    Esther Wyndham

☐ **VOLUME XXVI**
527 RETURN TO LOVE, Alex Stuart
621 NURSE TO CAPTAIN ANDY,
    Jill Christian
656 STORMY HAVEN, Rosalind Brett

☐ **VOLUME XXVII**
576 SANDFLOWER, Jane Arbor
626 NURSE TRENT'S CHILDREN,
    Joyce Dingwell
782 INHERIT MY HEART,
    Mary Burchell

☐ **VOLUME XXVIII**
542 CITY OF DREAMS, Elizabeth Hoy
651 DANGEROUS OBSESSION,
    Jean S. Macleod
855 UNTIL WE MET, Anne Weale

☐ **VOLUME XXIX**
525 NURSE ELLIOT'S DIARY,
    Kate Norway
620 WHITE DOCTOR, Celine Conway
784 WHERE NO ROADS GO,
    Essie Summers

☐ **VOLUME XXX**
587 HEART SPECIALIST, Susan Barrie
633 CHILDREN'S NURSE,
    Kathryn Blair
896 CHILD FRIDAY, Sara Seale

To: Harlequin Reader Service, Dept. G.
    M.P.O. Box 707, Niagara Falls, N.Y. 14302
    Canadian address: Stratford, Ont., Canada

☐ Please send me complete listing of the 30 Golden Harlequin
  Library Volumes.

☐ Please send me the Golden Harlequin Library editions I
  have indicated above.

I enclose $............... (No C.O.D.'s) To help defray postage
and handling costs, please add 50c.

Name ....

Address ....

City/Town ....

State/Province .... Zip ....

M